A LIFE GIVEN,
A LIFE TAKEN

By

Francis Voignier

AN AUTOBIOGRAPHY

Cover design by Francis Voignier
Licensed *iStock* image, tawanlubfah © 2019

Although this book is a work of fiction, it is immersed in the private experience; consequently, names have been substituted to protect the privacy of living individuals. Their replacements are by no means to be confused with real people unassociated with this story.

Library of Congress Cataloging-in-Publication Data
Voignier, Francis 1954—United States
A Life Given, a Life Taken/Francis Voignier
ISBN-13: 9781952858017
ISBN-10: 1952858011

Fiction – Biography – Rock & Roll – Philosophy – Psychology

francisvoignier.com
Dolosse & Writs, Eureka, CA

LIST OF CONTENTS

1 – BROKEN ROOTS

I wake up. My eyes won't open. I still hear the sweet music. Tomaso Albinoni's Adagio.

I wake up again. Behind the four blue walls of the crib—a scraping noise. Behind the noise—the devil's hand, red and black and menacing. I scream. I run to the safety of the kitchen, hysterical. Mama is busy with burnt and twisted matches spread on the open oven door. It smells of gas and sulfur. She looks beautiful in her floral dress, but I shake—terrorized. She doesn't know what's wrong with me.

I stand in the middle of the garden. Something warm and lumpy fills my diapers. I awaken to self-consciousness and discomfort. It won't happen again.

I stand in the garden. I can barely hold the incoming bowel. The red plastic pail calls. I shit in it and show the feat to Papa, satisfied with the accomplishment. He takes it to Mama. I hear hearty laughter from behind the wood stack. I feel complete.

I don't speak—I think.

I dislike the garden and the row of rabbit cages. I dislike the house—the devil lives in it. There are many things I don't like, but I know not what they are, except for grapes.

I sit in the high chair eyeing the grapes on my plate. I never had them, but they're definitely evil. I hate grapes with a passion! Mama forces one against my clenched teeth. I scream, I fight to the death, flailing arms and legs. The plate breaks on the floor, grapes roll around the kitchen. Mama is mad. With a final, determined push, a grape explodes in my mouth, its juice running down my chin, along my neck, down my chest, and also down my throat. I freeze. Sweet nectar. I love grapes!

I don't know how I know it, but I'm one year old—Mama's twenty-one—whatever that means.

I love the house across the road—a big house hidden behind tall trees. I know about secrets and mystery—not in my head, but in a place between my beating heart and my belly. That house is full of mystery—I want to live in it.

I walk between Mama and Papa. We stop each time they speak with the big ones. They call me Jewel. I don't care about names because I don't understand why we have to have them. Jewel sounds like something I'm not allowed to lose, but I will lose it like I lose everything. I don't know expectation but I know what it feels like. I still don't talk, save for the bare essentials, like when I want grapes. But I think in big words. And colors. And hopes—impossible ones.

There is trouble between Mama and Papa. There's also trouble between Mama and those I can't see. That's why I stay with Grandma and Grandpa, but there's trouble there too.

Mama is back. She's happy for a day then she screams again.

Grandma and Grandpa live in darkness. There's a hole in the floor that leads to the dirt basement, where potatoes, carrots, and onions live—a scary place. It smells like old people in very old houses, dry, powdery, musty—not a bad smell, but not a cheerful one either. I sleep with grandma in a closet. I didn't know people slept in closets, but they do when they get old. Grandpa sleeps elsewhere because he gets up in the middle of the night to go to work. Work doesn't seem like fun. I can tell, because when Papa and Grandpa come back from the factory, they are mute and their eyes look into unhappy places. The factory must be Hell! I know of Hell and the devil; it's always lurking like something that has been following me—like the music.

I wonder why Grandma and Grandpa keep their shutters close when it's light outside. They also dress in black. Old people like black.

Grandpa went to War when he was young. War sounds like a faraway place. One day, I'll go to War too.

Grandma's gone. A *hit of the blood*, they say, but her heart refuses to stop. I don't know how people die with a beating heart—it sounds silly. But Grandpa isn't amused. He's skin and bones, diminished in the blackness of his sorrow inside his black clothes. I know it's not a happy time, but I feel happy, even though Grandma is gone in the head. I know she's in a happy place with lots of light.

At the funeral, I learn Grandma was born on a canal boat, somewhere in old Bavaria, or maybe farther east, like the Austrian Empire.

I am now four. It's 1958 and the second big war is still with us like a shadow. I decide I will never go to war. War isn't a place.

Mama is an orphan of war, which doesn't mean my other Grandma and Grandpa died in it. No, Mama was an orphan before it started. That's why she screams, and when the screaming can't stop, the ambulance comes to take her away.

I love the redhead keeping an eye on us at kindergarten; she's so much nicer than the nuns that run the place. The Belgian one's short and skinny, with hair protruding from her chin. She says it's a mortal sin to spit in the font, as a speck of her spittle hits the holy water. I tell her she's going to Hell. She screams and hits.

I have two sisters—one's a baby. When Mama's away, we sometimes visit on the weekend. She smiles, but she can't walk because she's too tired. They give her electroshock. I was shocked once—it's no fun.

I talk a lot, they say. All the words push each other in my head. Sometimes, I don't say the right thing, but I don't mean to. I get slapped in the face for it—it hurts a lot. But that's still better than the whip, which comes out more and more and for no reason. I guess I lost the jewel I wasn't supposed to lose.

Grandpa moved to a room on the back side of the castle. We, my sisters and I with the parents, moved at the base of it, on the other side. I love the castle with its mysterious figures all clad in iron. The chatelaine is kind enough to have us kids on regular visits. I love the big shiny copper pots of the stone kitchen, and the stairs going up and around the towers. We also get candy—the good kind.

My Godmother and uncle visit on my birthday. I run up the street towards their parked car, shouting, "I'm five, I'm five!"

"Don't be so impolite!" she scolds me.

I don't know what impolite means, so I ask, "Do you mean 'polite'?"

She's angry with me. I was happy—now I'm not so sure.

I have this little red scooter. I go down the steep, unpaved street, beaming with joy. Suddenly, I stop. The world comes to an end. I feel like I'm dying an atrocious death; not a painful death, but from something much worse going on in my head. I can't breathe, I start shaking, my heart beats too fast—a horrific sense of loneliness enrobes me in its dark cloak. I'm so scared, as I fall into a vortex of nothingness, meaninglessness, absurd abstraction. The big words in my thoughts. Mother doesn't know what to do with me, but she feels my pain—she understands it, the panic, the trauma, the brutal alienation. I was five a minute ago, now I feel the weight of ages. Slowly, I calm down, and then it starts all over again, every hour of day and night for weeks, for months, for years...

I'm six and I'm top of my class. I don't learn—I improvise my way through methodological teaching, extracting knowledge from the root of my being. Big words again—I can't stop them from knocking at the door. Maybe they're not words, just word forms. I don't care one way or the other—I won't follow the rules. But it costs me because doing nothing to reach number one insults numbers two and three—the big competitors. I get picked on, but with caution.

I spend more time with Grandpa. He has moved again, this time, in an even darker place with a single shuttered window. He eats hardly at all; he's a ghost looking into an empty world, but he's there for me through the devastating sadness.

Mother is back, and so are my sisters. We take turns being whipped for being children. The pain is unbearable. The joy is slowly and steadily extracted out of us until our hearts are blackened. Mother's screaming is incessant.

I don't know why there's a sink in my bedroom, but under it, I find a magazine full of pictures of naked women. Something happens inside me. I suddenly become aware of my gender.

Grandpa isn't well. They take him to the hospital: stomach cancer and tuberculosis. He dies soon, weighing eighty-five pounds. I don't miss him; there was no love there, just misery. I've got my own misery to deal with, but I don't let it out for anyone; not even for mother who's dealing with her own nightmares.

I cough incessantly. I cough blood.

I'm on a train to the mountains. Father leaves me with two nuns who take me away. I'm scared and lonely.

Grandpa's gift before parting: tuberculosis.

I meet the Devil once again, at the foot of my bed, at three in the morning. My screams wake the night nurse up and many patients. I'm horrified at my own self, humiliated, alone, and horribly frightened.

The three and a half hour afternoon nap takes forever. I'm not tired; I want to run—they tie me to the bed.

Maybe it's the drugs, but the pangs have subsided for a while. I'm being pumped with penicillin among pills and shots of I don't know what. Too many white cells, they say. I can only surrender.

My best friend is sixteen—I'm seven. He makes me feel strong and brave, because I know he's strong and brave—and kind. He's an angel. We wait in line for the weekly blood test. I know he won't cry, so I won't either, even if it hurts like mad. Before long, he's gone and I'm lonely again.

More forced sleep, more drugs. I can't sleep—I'm about to explode.

Finally, I'm no longer a threat to the world. Father picks me up. It's been six months since I last saw him.

Mother is happy to see me. We're a family of a few days then the screaming and the beating resume. I return to school, and to my surprise, I'm still number one; even after having missed half a year. Two and three couldn't catch up with my lead. I know they hate me and so do their parents, especially the mothers. They don't hide their feelings either. "Little asshole!" one spits. It hurts and it doesn't. I'm in feeling-assessing mode.

They say I'm smart and deft with cards. I win most games. They think I don't know what they think.

They think they're letting me win because I'm supposed to lack adult intelligence. I don't want them to know what I think about adult intelligence, because that would be more trouble than it's worth.

I'm eight and I'm still top of the class. All from barely glancing at books. I don't even own the right ones, because the parents... it's a long story. The teacher's wife teaches the next class, so the couple, either out of curiosity or for the sake of amusement, decides to move me to the seniors' final test. I pass handily. They look astonished since there are no multiple choices. They ask how I know the answers—I have no answer for that.

It's the family's last year in town, I hear. I'm the uncontestable number one. The school director, upon granting me my prize, endeavors to slap me in the face in front of students and parents. "This is for your effrontery! Maybe, one day, you'll have the decency to study like the rest of us before you can take top honors!" I'm appalled! I feel humiliated and angry—the kind of toxic anger that eats at my core. Fuck him! Fuck school! Fuck fucking parents, and teachers, and all the fucking stupid kids built in their image—fuck them all!

It's summer—school's forgotten. The parents have sent me to camp—I'm free! I love everyone around me. I'm also in love with a blonde and a brunette— valiant love. I dream of saving them from harm—I'm a knight, I'm a dragon slayer!

2 – DESCENT

We move. The family, that is. Part of me stays behind to take care of unfinished business. I say goodbye.

It's hot. Father drinks wine—he shouldn't. He's in a frenzy verging on madness. I know he's dangerous like when he tried to kill me once and broke his foot instead. Just as predicted, drama makes its stage entrance—father gets his hand crushed by the swing of the moving truck door. Someone takes him to the hospital. I'm now the passenger—the truck driver drinks wine from a bottle as he wrestles pedals and sticks amid the grinding of gears. He stinks of alcohol—he, too, is a dangerous man.

I'm in fear—I'm always in fear. Something snaps. Father scares the living hell out of me, and Mother's screaming is finally turning my nerves to shreds. What's left of my confidence is changing into something that scares me even more—lies. Lies for the sake of protection, lies to buy time, lies to distract and confuse. Lies are dangerous, but they're the only weapon left against the blows. I dislike what I've become. It's not me out there; he's a fake, but I'm afraid to come out and reclaim the space, the wasteland of broken promises, injustice, torment...

I'm no longer top of the class. I don't care—fuck school!

Mother sends me to catechism. The vicar's a vicious beast that preys on young boys, just like the nuns prey on young girls, according to my sisters. I want to kill him from the time he dragged me on the floor by my ears and made me squeal like a slaughtered pig. Poison darts it is! But there are hurdles like when I dreamed of building a bicycle out of sticks an old rubber tires. But the bastard will die one way or the other!

I hate church service. I guess that with so many visits from Satan, it comes naturally. But I love churches because they're mysterious, like the meaning of life, which has been on my mind since I first encountered death on my little red scooter five years ago. The vicar doesn't know the meaning of life in spite of all the religion behind him. Actually, no-one seems to know the meaning of life, not from my perspective. Yet, the adults act like they have it all figured out. But I know better; not the priest or the doctor, not religion or science, not the thinkers or the arrogance of knowledge can tell me the meaning of life. Not even the composers and the players, even when it brushes them by through the many voices of music.

I love classical music—I've got a list of all the composers and their work. Every day, I listen to the classical station. I'm sure the meaning of life is in there somewhere. But then, when I'm alone, I also listen to Gene Vincent, Eddie Cochran, Jerry Lee Lewis—music for the longing down below. I'm confused between the deep calmness of the soul and the restless churning in my guts. I abhor my position.

I play the recorder. The teacher quizzes us about what we know about music. I suggest the work of Adam de la Halle. He takes offense. I'm punished with the task of writing about the early composer. Somehow, I don't think he knows who he is. Here it goes again!

I hand the music teacher my paper on Adam de la Halle. He doesn't look at it; instead, he tears it to pieces and throws it in the trash. Something cries deep inside.

It's obvious people are mean—the world is mean. The neighbors are full of spite, telling on each other, lying about each other. Everybody lies. It no longer matters if I do, but I still feel like a fake—we're all fakes.

School festers with reasons for anxiety. The German teacher, Mrs. Wolf, is a mean bitch. The French teacher is a pedantic giraffe with cat eye glasses and high, pointy breasts. The science teacher, a short, athletic, bearded man, has a temper as short as his looks, and hands prone to hitting faces in vicious, cracking slaps. The director is a tall and ugly old man with a protruding belly. He wears a black suit, drives a black car, and the sky always darkens when I get called to his office.

Getting called to the director's office means my lies have reached their expiry dates. Father is never far behind with punishment. I'm surrounded by monsters.

I'm in love with one of the girls, but she never looks at me. Love is weird.

I go through the hell of Solemn Communion, fake smile et al. The parents are filled with pride—me, with embarrassment. They're not even religious, the fucking bastards! Any which way to keep me out of their hair is fair game to them, so I'm on to Confirmation, or else... I enjoy being away from them, but not in the company of the vicar. I so want to grow up—fast!

Mother cuts her wrists—she survives. Mother is found with her head inside the gas range, her lungs and blood streams full of butane—she survives. Mother swallows a whole load of pills—she bloody survives. Can't she fucking die already?!

Father doesn't say much anymore. The screaming has gotten to him too. He hides his drinking in the privacy of the basement. He doesn't hit as much, but when he does, he hits harder, more viciously, more crazily, without any concern for the consequences. The voice of reason is mute. I die numerous times—almost. Father drinks to bury the guilt—he's a cornered beast.

My godmother gives me a guitar. Father threatens to toss it in the coal furnace. Another voice cries inside. I wish the Devil came around these days.

I take the guitar to the woods behind the house, play to the trees, one difficult note at a time—do, re, mi... I play to the cows in the pastures—E minor, A minor... I share what I learn with a couple of new friends. Guitars help in making fast friends—guitars help in bringing girls out of their mysterious, hidden places. Parents hate guitars—parents hate long hair. Adults loathe change!

My English teacher's the best. I adore him. He speaks my language. Funny how that sounds! He smells of London, umbrellas, bowler hats, double-deckers, tea and crumpets. I so want to move to London!

I'm in Normandy, across the channel from England. Me and a friend ran away from camp; the plan is to steal a boat and row to the cliffs of Dover. We've got the geography wrong, across is the Isle of Wight. Anyway, the cops are on us.

It's not a fun time to be twelve, surrounded by a plethora of evils. The meaning of life becomes oh so elusive, pulling away in shreds from my broken nails. The pangs turn to the dullness of overdone hurt. I contemplate the way out, but I want it to mean something, to teach and punish in the grand style of martyrdom. Like Jesus. But the vicar killed Jesus, Mary, and all the saints. He might as well have killed me too.

Death is never too far, in fear or in hope. The two faces of drama flicker randomly, never surrendering to the mood. It's a cat and mouse chase—a race to ever-so-distant emotional safety.

There's a world outside within which I partake with the obligatory flexing. I play my part with adequate conviction. Music is the common denominator to inner and outer realities. It satisfactorily conceals the answer-seeking ghost behind it. With it, I'm one of them—without it, no-one sees me. But all's blurry, unreal. The true focus is on tone and melody. I write my first three songs, each a little savior, each a part of the meaning of life.

As much as I love classical, my focus is on rock and roll, the dark and angry kind. It's a long way from

Vivaldi or old Adam de la Halle, but we're in the nineteen-sixties. It's all about catching the wind.

Somehow, the vicar takes on liking me. We go to the country in his black sedan; he, robed in more black with a big silver cross on his chest; me, crawling out of my skin with the reinforced sense of not belonging—I rarely belong.

Questions abound, but I move along. After the vicar drops me in some alien town, I buy my first pack of smokes with my daily food allowance. I'm here because of the fucking confirmation, the indelible mark of Christianity—it's a charade!

It's like school but worse. I'm distracted and I learn nothing of the posturing—I'm fully unprepared for the ceremony. After the anointment, I will carry with joy the responsibility of unveiling to man and world the love of God. Someone have mercy!

It's the ceremony—I improvise. I take my turn to face the bishop, fragrant oil on my forehead—I'm done!

No joy fills the parents this time. No pride. Father looks at me with a murderous stare. Yesterday, they met with the school director when I was still away. I'm glad I smoked all those cigarettes.

Religion's out of the way—good riddance! It's camp time again. Oh no, another vicar and an abbot from the next town over are running the show—I'm doomed!

Strangely, they dress casual, play guitar, tell stories, and pass cigarettes; and not once do they mention

God or the Devil. Six weeks with two priests, yet no service, no sermon, no talk of sin and punishment. Who are these men that come from nowhere, spend six weeks in my sphere of reality, and go on to never be seen again? The winds are turning. I arrive wounded and leave healed.

I find Heaven, and religion isn't in it.

I see the light for the first time since my encounter with the void eight years ago. The world is beautiful without rules and the will of men and women of spite. It has scent, vibrancy, language; its apples, sweet nectar, unlike the bitter of those grown in an Eden imagined by the wickedness of sick minds.

I then discover the meaning of irony.

As the pangs recede, so does my desire to find the meaning of life. Life has no meaning, that's all! It's a minute by minute improvisation across a mine field of parent props—distorted, derisive, drunken, and above all, extremely dumb and proportionally mean. A few of the adults are kind, but they don't exist in my close environment—they're too smart for that!

Musicians aren't adults—they never age.

The Beatles are OK as long as it's *I'm Down, Dizzy Miss Lizzy*, and *Hey Bulldog*. Otherwise, I much prefer the Pretty Things. Faddy headlines are for people who don't know my kind of pain. The Pretty Things or the Troggs know what I'm talking about.

It's not all about music, though music is a big part of why I'm still sane. No, the bigger part is about Mother's screaming and the ongoing flurry of slaps in the face, Father's brutish approach to bonding—the "what doesn't kill you makes you stronger" motto of those most needing of psychological help. Tough love? You've got to be kidding!

About psychology, or, in this case, psychiatry rather, the parents deem my behavior worthy of adjustment, that is: medication. Somehow, I knew it would come to that. It takes no genius to figure out the logical path from denial to blame. I don't have the word for it, but it's like the "narcissism of dementia"—it's all about them in a game of the absurd. I watch for signs of it in myself; godlessness forbids I should become one of them! Anyway, the psychiatrist goes through the motions then asks Mother to leave the room. He turns to me and says, "Sorry, kid, I don't know how to put it to you, but there's nothing wrong with you—it's your parents that belong here—and you know, I'm sure, there's no way of convincing them of it. Keep that to yourself, will ya, and stay true."

Help comes in mysterious ways.

3 – THE SPIRAL

Now that it's not just me saying there's something wrong with my immediate environment, I can move on—unimpeded.

I'm at the age at which the line defining the necessity of being parented becomes blurred. I intuit that by now, other species would have sent me on my sweet way to survival of the fittest.

I'm stronger in the face of torment, but by no means is said torment relenting in its onslaught. Father, in feeding on his own misery, is all the more dangerous. It doesn't mean he doesn't have good spells, but they're never to be trusted. The flip-flopping of tragicomedy lives vibrant in my zone of self-defense. Mother dares another throw of hand at my face, instead her wrist is held captive by the vise of my fingers to the tone of, "You do that again and you're dead—get it?!" She flies, shouting bloody murder to a street audience of indifference. She won't slap me again, but the screaming goes on.

It's the era of long band names, ours is *Nuclear Power Station*, won in a toss against the German *Lichtelektrische Zelle*. My amp is an old tube radio with an oval speaker—one watt of pure glory. It's a garage concert with a generous serving of "nothing rehearsed." We make money selling a couple of cases of beer, courtesy the stash of some unsuspecting parent. I know we stink, but a step's a step. I think I'm drunk—desensitized from the world around me. Minutes become hours without warning. Shit's awaiting me at home.

Home is where the heart is, they say. Whose heart—the heart of what? Had I survived the crash landing of my planned birth ten years prior, my heart would presently be in London—simple as that! Fuck yeah! Get it, you up there, whoever you are?!

I run, I can't stop running. I practically fly—I'm that fast. And yet, I never fall. I'd love to own a bicycle, but until then, I'll keep on running.

War planes streak the sky like banshees chased by thunder. There's a conflict in the Middle East, Israel against Syria, Jordan, and Egypt. Grownups big on strategy fear the worst. I know they love it, but they pretend they don't. Lies. I long for a war that'd put an end to my torments and set me free. One bomb on the neighborhood—poof! I'd survive and prosper. I'm told such wishes are evil. I know, but I'm just cashing in.

There're the girls, but nothing comes of it. They're prisoners like my sisters are. My heart swells and deflates at the rate of a stolen kiss that never comes. Love exists in side glances and corner smiles, promises of better days ahead that seem to end in unwanted pregnancies for some of the older ones. A quick kiss on the lips would do for now, or just the thrill of a first name. The world gets stranger with every discovery, every bit of news. People die around me, mostly for the better, but some of my age leave too; it's not sad—just odd. I realize I observe more than I identify. I guess there's too much pain in playing the game—life's much safer from the outside when no-one can see you.

It's funny that hiding doesn't necessarily require hiding—it's all a state of mind. Invisibility is a skill developed by those who've been in the crosshair for too long. There's nothing to it when you've met the prerequisites. I imagine it's a lot tougher for those who think that the art of not being seen lies in the acquisition of special abilities found amid the bazaars of private chimeras. Invisibility is borne of intellectual and emotional disconnection with one's environment—not of severing perception as one might think.

Talking of awareness, thirteen's about the age of one coming into their own: self-awareness as opposed to brainlessness and knee-jerking. I'm starting to see where the meaning of life has been escaping the many. Awareness infers the freedom to manœuver around the self— without it, there's no meaning to living. And yet, the vast majority within my sphere of experience live without a modicum of self-awareness. Their version of it is reflexive bordering on narcissistic. It's about pitting the self against others, about gain, control, and power; all of it all the more aggravated by the inability to exist in the present; hence the vicious blows onward to savage what they can't attain: smarts, accomplishment, and inner peace.

I'm just letting the thoughts go. Obviously, I don't know inner peace, but I could use some right now. I barely know self-awareness—it's all new to me—but I'm on it.

It's all nice and dandy, but adversity is always on the menu—invisibility or not. Injustice prevails and with it the fears and the loss of self-confidence.

Confidence is essential to building status; without it one exists in a state of arrested development. Forget about impressing the girls—they can't see you.

I discover table tennis. *Penny Lane* plays in the background. Actually, Mother, in her back-handed way of doing such things as creating space for herself, signed me up for it. It's a lot better than catechism and exponentially more useful.

I'm good at it. It's like running without the distance. But I have a problem with winning games the minute they count. I kill at practice and fall apart during competition. My guts turn to jelly—I feel sick the second my name's on the line—too much exposure and self-expectation. And that sucks!

But not all is lost—getting better at playing the guitar brings on the private confidence of specialization. I'm the only serious musician within a mile radius and that counts. Of course, zero competition!

It's a cousin's wedding—I discover the effects of drinking wine and beer in a sequential, upward swing of unbelievable confidence turned bravado, turned "I feel invincible," immediately followed by a loss of body functions, culminating in my guts being wringed until all vomit, phlegm, and whatever else pool in a colorful stench by the side of some country road. A cow looks at me before I collect my scattered wits and wander into oblivion.

The morning feels like a jackhammer clamped between my ears. Father reminds me of how I distinguish myself as the asshole in the family, but his words sound reasonable compared to the living nightmare of my first hangover. At least he doesn't beat me, which I take as something akin to a form of bonding in regard to general male assholery.

Mother, on the other hand, doesn't even deign knowing me—her false pride shattered by my antics. The woman of few subtleties playacts moral silence—what happened to the screaming?

By the way, Mother's pregnant. I hear it's a chance in a thousand she'll reach delivery. Of course, it comes as an unscheduled burden—an act of God of sorts. Perhaps all are expecting her to miscarriage like she did half dozen times in a row. From where I stand, she's not going to because I was there most of the times when she bled all over and she's looking a lot healthier now. Actually, in one heart-wrenching moment of pure connectivity between us, she once took me to the side to explain what to do if she were to lose the baby, which consisted mostly of running to the public phone and calling the doc—I was ten then.

Brother joins us in the middle of the worst family freeze-over. Who's this thing, and who's gonna take care of it—certainly not Mother or Father. No breast milk for the little guy; it's straight to formula! It's not like Mother has lost her mammary functions, no, she can't bother; plus it's too close for comfort. I wonder how Father managed to squeak one past her guards. The thought nauseates me.

So, since my sisters are pretty useless, I get to watch the "thing." It's tough to go from a rebellious rock and roll frame of mind to babysitting. I feel rather humiliated, but then, imagine being in the little guy's shoes... What in the world did he do to land with us, the most dysfunctional family on this side of the steel mill?

Karma sucks!

At least, I now have a defined function: parenting. Life is full of sick jokes that even Coyote puts disclaimers on. But I bear my cross and keep an eye on the neonate.

If I shan't provide warmth to the kid, I shall provide tunes—my best shot at giving a shit. There's magic in having him shut up and go to sleep to my serenading. I give him formula, change the diapers, take him out on wild stroller adventures inclusive of all-terrain stunts—the life. He seems to enjoy my shenanigans, and with it, I'm starting to appreciate our time together, since it provides ample freedom, which ironically coincides with the parents relishing not having to deal with him. I swear; irony never sleeps!

I've never been much into the Beatles, but *Magical Mystery Tour* has my attention—and so does Hendrix. Forget singles, albums are the real deal! I must mention one song that turned me around a year or so ago: *Good Vibrations* by the Beach Boys. Brother, for not being my kind of band, those guys sure hit the nail on the head! Even rebels get to have a soft spot for something beautiful occasionally. Mind you, I was born with an adagio that has been droning in the background my entire life, so I know beautiful when it brushes by.

By the look of it, *Nuclear Power Station* is no more—an early dismissal caused by some of the members' other commitments, notably, a lack of interest in music. There's something interesting in the way passions die from the lack of instant gratification. The fickleness of the human mind befuddles the observer of life. I guess it takes a dream to accept patience and perseverance as both hurdles and allies.

My namesake friend gets an actual allowance to build his record collection. Me, I get nothing, not even for babysitting my kid brother. That's how I get to hear *Piper at the Gates of Dawn* and myriad gems by obscure bands, which is the next best thing to owning my own collection, and far better than hearing nothing at all. So, thanks to him for the many sessions of sacred listeningness. On a balanced note, he's got someone with whom to share who actually adores the stuff, as opposed to the generalness of bleak feeding on pop music out there. It makes sense we're friends.

I sneak choreographed outings to the big city to assist my mate in selecting new music, but the parents get wind of it and axe my newborn freedom, embarrassing me in the process. Now, I'm on double duty with the baby. Talking of karma, I'm starting to believe that my plate was full on arrival, which doesn't help assuaging the existentiality of my experience. I'm spiraling downwards into the bowels of a reality bereft of sanity and hope. I imagine the parents being some sort of hired hit team; the mastermind, an old archenemy full of acrimony, seeing to the particular details of my misery. If Death didn't scare me, I would gladly clasp her bony hand and let her take me back home.

The blows come and go in rhythm with the screaming. I should make it clear that the beating doesn't happen without it, while the screaming wanes when Father's gone. Individually, the parents are far from being as bad as their joined selves. The recipe's pretty simple; they hate each other and we, the kids, are left to be the punching bags to their frustrations—kinda typical judging by the neighborhood. So, yes, victims of abuse abound amid proletarian reality, and it doesn't take a rocket scientist to link the contributing elements to the general misery. Husbands overwork for the man, underpaid, under a rule of blackmail and fear, while the wives and kids agonize to the sounds of the steps announcing their returns. I hear of a family whose mother and daughters piss their knickers daily just from hearing those steps. I have no clue as to what goes on in that house, but I consider myself lucky to not live in it. The odd thing about my pad is that Father fears Mother—a distinction I ought to be proud of.

It is with points of reference such as the ones depicting far worse cases that I find redemption. Life tells us that there's always worse (as well as better) than imagined—extremes are elusive.

But that doesn't really change anything, since I was born with the idea that better is the way to look for, and not the other way round. So, while I hope for better, I realize that the whole concept is subjective. I think everybody suffers and finds happiness under their own rules; it's just that there's a threshold that mustn't be crossed. You can suffer from being spoiled, but you can hardly be spoiled from suffering—humbled at best perhaps, ruined or erased at worst. So, there's a nuance in perception here, and I trust it defines itself in the dual violation of bodily and psychological savagery.

What I mean by dysfunctional is that we, as a family, missed on the opportunity to be functional. There are hopeless cases out there that never have a go at functionality, so it's hard to call them dysfunctional. No, put simply, my parents threw their chances at parenthood away, opting instead to cater to the child within as opposed to the children without. The tragedy lies in the rebuttal of potential, when, as to others, it does in the ignorance of it—all this to say that my parents aren't hopeless morons. Which brings me to wonder why they choose to be total assholes when they well know they don't have to, or worse, don't really want to—hence the guilt.

The case defies common sense, but there lies the fine line between sane and mental. Mother's insane; it's well documented. After all, her best war memory is of being fed by an enemy soldier—that sums up five years worth of love. As to Father, I've got no idea what makes him so mad with rage. Him, I can't excuse.

I don't fear Mother; she just drives me crazy, but Father scares the living hell out of me, every bloody day of the week!

So yes, I just turn thirteen and things aren't getting any better, in spite of me trying to see the silver lining. I just hope the future will bring something nice for a change.

1968 is a mess. A general strike, no open schools, endless demonstrations, barricades, Molotov cocktails, big union talks/small results, political standoffs, and military shenanigans populate the list. It's a good time to sneak sorties when the parents are preoccupied.

Personally, I find the times exciting, exhilarating, full of promise—like two springs in one.

It's also when rock and roll takes a turn to something a lot harder than flowers in your hair. The term heavy metal makes so much sense in metallurgical reality—we breathe sulfurous fumes; ingest mercury; drink lead, cadmium, phosphorus; get our eyeballs and lungs speared by rust darts falling from billowing red clouds. Paradoxically, it's also California, land of hippies and the Grateful Dead, that brings us heavy metal. Extra long hair and loudness define true kickass rebellion— Blue Cheer steals my heart.

Unfortunately, distraction isn't enough to keep me safe. Desperate times call for desperate measures, and there's no better time than those to pretend the family is a close unit that must stick together for survival. And what better time it is to release frustration in novel ways! I want nothing of it, while the parents, supported by the illusion that all ends justify the means, take advantage of the no-holds-barred principles of punishment. There are no rewards for the creativeness of abuse, yet some are drawn to its unseen glory. It leaves me with the question, "What does one gain from being an all-out asshole?" The lack of visibility seems to encourage despicable acts only witnessed by the rare sadistic onlooker. It's like a one on one affair that begs for the poetry of justice to set the stage for retribution. It's simple; one day, when all the pain and frustration gets to recognize they now exist in a strong enough body, I shall give back to Father what's due to him; hoping I'll arrange to not downright kill him.

In a display reminiscent of what happened in school a few years back, I'm handed a verdict that stinks of favoritism. In spite of having aced the final exam—although, in all honesty, I didn't do much for it—I'm sentenced to grade retention, courtesy the math teacher who took insult at my high score following a dismal year. My aim's to pass with minimal effort; unfortunately some see it as a con. Somehow, there's always someone who takes affront at something that doesn't concern them. I'm furious, and the parent even more so. But instead of going after the teacher, the cowards zoom on me with renewed vitality. As if the humiliation wasn't enough, now I must endure torture.

Needless to say, I've had my share of educational upheavals. I'm looking at a wasted year in a wasteland of moral privation, defeated and utterly heartbroken.

I bear my cross with the resilience of those who bear crosses as if it were mere exercise, but there's an end to endurance, and the end is near. Fundamentally, I wish nothing but the best to all. Externally, the mood is on vengeance, misdeed, and Machiavellian schemes. It's also on how to get the fuck out of Dodge.

 I realize I'm poorly equipped to survive on my own while evading the law, so leaving the house will require sophistication. In the meantime, the end of the year is abuzz with some of the greatest music I've ever been able to relate to: the *White Album* by the Beatles, Deep Purple's *Shades of Deep Purple*, Jeff Beck's *Truth*, etcetera. *Helter Skelter*, oh my!

 I want to do drugs like hash and acid, but they're out of my reach, so I sneak the occasional cigarette and beer instead.

 I discover masturbation, which adds a welcome quality to my life—a life made of layers, as I perceive with astonishment. The emotional qualitative of hormonal charges is something to behold. With late puberty comes dimension, particularly in the appreciation of the laws of attraction. Girls turn to Goddesses, and a stolen kiss is no longer enough when fantasy takes the mind into the eroticism of a desert island for two.

 Back to reality, my thoughts and heart are preoccupied with my first female friend, making all the previous "serious" encounters with the neighborhood girls dull in comparison. She's two years older, but I'm her guitar teacher, which makes us even. She's tall, slim, dyes her hair henna-black, wears a leather jacket, black jeans, and combat boots. She's special to the tune of no-one like her exists in the perceivable universe. I'm beyond in love, but the miracle lies in a quality that only us two share—a sense of equality that keeps sex at bay, leaving plenty of room to appreciate life around a cup of espresso.

There's no fantasy of secret islands with the two of us conveniently stranded. No, the present suffices—the fantasy is real—here, right across me, sits the most beautiful female I ever laid my eyes on, and she smiles at me with unrestrained complicity.

Never mind the parents, teachers, academia, competition... all meaningless. There's only the present, and the present is all the more vivid with this Goddess in it. Problem is, she's moving in a month to a far away city. I promise to myself I will always love her. And so I find, with a mix of amusement and resignation, that joy and tears can cohabit.

With my love gone, I'm here to reflect on my situation. I still take care of little brother, but my sisters are becoming increasingly aware he exists, so help's on the way. Something that shames me and has done so for some time is the fact I'm practically a housekeeper on top of all the other stuff. I mop and wax the floors, dust the furniture, wash and dry the dishes, make the beds, iron and fold the clothes; shirts, sheets, undies, towels, diapers, pants, dresses... all stacked in neat piles to replenish the shelves. As I said before, the sisters are useless; and where's Mother when she's needed?

I've always felt taken advantage of. Obviously nothing has changed—I'm the floor mat, the servant, the slave... and therein lies the discomfort of low self-esteem.

The familial life is the great vacuum, the downdraft of all things decent and meaningful, the affront to the creative spirit, and above all, the death of the natal ego. It's the unlearning process that takes one from the vertex of knowledge to the lows of ignorance. No-one should be born into potential to end up shackled, and yet, there isn't a wiser way to describe my rebirth into awareness—I live in a stone cell whose space of forests, fields, and seas, beyond its walls, is merely the byproduct of illusion—ever present, albeit unattainable.

Now that neither the Devil nor Death deign surprise me with their visits, I wish to die.

4 – CORSICA

I'm atop the ship taking me from Marseille to Bastia, Corsica. I'm free for the next six weeks. The sea is swollen and the skies are full with ominous signs. Porpoises follow in pods as seagulls flock above in random, broken flights. The winds pick up, lifting the surf in great bursts of splashes all the way to the top deck. I endeavor to slide along its wet floor, pushed by the gusts, clear to its end and back again. It's dangerous, but no-one's around to tell me so. Soon, the ship heaves as a million whips lash from the descending blackness. I'm drenched but happy, cleansed from all things sticky and malfeasant—the toxicity of social and familial injustice scrubbed away by the might of the elements. I'm one with the rightful rage of nature, cocooned by its fury, released from the dullness of insignificance.

In their rush to create space for themselves, the parents unwisely sent me to camp in heaven, aka the Island of Beauty. It's an all-boy affair of fifteen to eighteen year olds, but it's obvious the elders are far more than boys. They have confidence, wisdom, and some manhood below the belt. I'm definitely intimidated, but once again, the guitar comes to the rescue.

It's unreported how much difference there actually is between the bottom and the top of that small age group. Those three years encompass the transition from boyhood to adulthood, as I see it—something that applies more to males than females as observed, but for which I lack the science. For example, my Goddess friend, last year, was more of an adult at sixteen than some grownups in their twenties. It's all figurative, though. Thinking of her, I wouldn't hesitate to swap my time in paradise for some with her around cappuccinos. I wonder how long it would have taken us before we fucked—not long, I trust. How my heart aches!

We set camp by an empty beach on the eastern side of the island. The instructors are almost as young as the elders in the group, so a certain mutual understanding prevails, meaning we can do whatever the fuck we want. We smoke, drink beer, loll around beach bum-style, play records on the lowly battery-powered player, eat out of cans, swim the warm waters... all of it under a radiant sun. The climax comes when we plan a week-long camping trip in the mountains that rise like an insurmountable wall, barely a mile west. Before long, the asphalt turns to dust as we pass ancient stone houses with their fallow grounds and distressed fruit trees, some almost dead. The rare cars pass us at insane speeds. Quick peeks into the ravines reveal that some of them never made it to their destinations. The top is a long way amid cacti and the dreaded maquis. We pass small villages that lay dormant in the mid-afternoon. Nothing's open, but municipal fountains gurgle with spring water to quench thirsts. The oversight remains irrelevant to insouciance. We make it to the end of the road by evening—the last village before the dust road becomes a thin trail into the heart of the mountains. Chicken and pigs roam the open sewage. We're granted permission to camp in a grove of chestnut trees, a small way up the path.

The one thing we're told is to never lie to the natives; the second, to respect the elders to the level of sacredness. In other words, a lack of courtesy towards them means death, and no-one will ever bother finding who did it. The book of rules is short and simple; you stick to it, you're one of them; you don't, goodbye!

I wonder what we're doing in contraband country where lawlessness is the only rule. I must admit there's comfort in it, a sense of belonging; nothing like I've ever been exposed to, or will be again. These people are free to exist whichever way they wish. I envy them.

Night is when things come to life in deep Corsica, as parties go well into dawn. Since any occasion is an opportunity for roasting a pig and toasting to good health, our presence is the perfect excuse to have one tomorrow. At once, all gears mesh into action. Fires are built, tables arranged, cured pigs are prepared and spitted ahead of their day-long roasting. By seven we're all gathered with food and drinks. French reverts to the native Italian—it hardly makes a difference when Johnny Walker Black Label sets the tone.

By midnight, everyone's drunk. The men shoot their guns in an endless fusillade, sending rippling echoes into the high mountains. I too am drunk, but many are the days since my initiative hangover. I'm stronger and smartened by the years.

The beach camp's alive with revisited stories of the hike, some more fantastic than others. What's remembered of those nights varies from one teller to the next—from mildly factual to phantasmagoric. It's all in the ratio of drinking to character. One thing's clear; when it comes to it, humans can't be trusted. Monsters turn to sheep just as quickly as sweetness turns to bile. Alcohol makes repression talk. I'm fairly sure one can repress goodness the same way one represses rage. You get the point.

It rains on the last day of camp, I take it it's a fitting homage to a stolen bit of happiness—it's all grey ahead.

As if on cue, the impossible happens. It's August 15th and it's snowing. I fear for my future.

Father abhors long hair—I want my hair long. In it lie the basic metrics of my relationship with him, which come with a flurry of blows that, instead of sending me crawling into a hole, make me more resolute to fight him at his own game. I don't budge, neither do I retaliate. The fury knows no bounds to the affront of silence, but every hit is a step backwards for poor, pathetic Father. Yes, I may die, yet defeated I shan't be.

With the help of now-panicked Mother, Father agrees to a compromise. I can have my hair long to a point, but forget the Dickie Peterson hairstyle. Pending patience, a baby step foretells a long stride.

Abbey road comes out, coincidentally becoming the numero uno album of my collection, courtesy the first money I ever make, setting pins at the outdoor bowling alley down the road. The second's *Kicking out the Jams*—beauty and the beast.

Not much's happening besides more playing and listening. Insubstantial infatuations come and go, missing at heeding the call of hormones. There's a mild paradox in girls coming to me red hot, to then go cold just when things become interesting. I practically "date" every female on the street, yet, with repeated predictability, each flips the switch at the same point, as if on cue. The dreaded erection does it every time; it's the breaker of spell, the master cooler. In the end, it makes no sense at all, unless of course, one dares venture into the psychology of survival. Unfortunately it's a big book I have neither the time nor the energy for reading and deciphering. Let's just say the girls are scared, and I wouldn't put it past a few fathers, some big brothers, and the occasional complicit mother to have embedded that fear inside them. Mouths speak and ears hear... Enough said!

My trip to Corsica has given me mojo—I think more clearly, define my surroundings with more precision, and reflect on the inner landscape with better perspective. As I already mentioned, the meaning of life is out of the picture at the mo; all is in dealing with what's available as it comes tumbling my way. Life's a stage; the script is experience in the making. As long as time and space want their share of the pie, linearity keeps me blind. The meaning will be defined in due absence of the continuum. It's a lot of thinking for a fifteen year old, but I have my sensors in many places since the parents failed at obliterating curiosity. I love science, especially physics, almost as much as I dig music, probably because I see how the two are linked. As to curiosity, it's universal, so no need to specialize when dealing with life—diversity broadens the mind.

The death pangs have practically become the stuff of forgetfulness, meaning that if I remember about them today, I most likely didn't yesterday, and mightn't tomorrow. It's not relief to forget; it's just nothing. When I remember; I reflexively stuff the thought back where it comes from, and then it's gone. I'm gonna be straight; the notion of them coming back frightens the life out of me, which is the nearest to them coming back. Although to live in them is quite different from the memory of living in them. Circles and figures of eight...

5 – EMOTIONAL UPHEAVAL

This year, instead of camp, I'm on a boat to Britain with a group of youth my age, half males and females. For the first time in a long time, there's the distinct possibility the parents are actually being genuinely generous. Not that it's costing them, since the mill's paying for it, but a generosity of mind nonetheless, as opposed to punishing me by keeping me stranded while my mates get all the fun visiting a place I've been dying of living in for as far as I can remember. But it didn't come without its share of blackmail, to which I did everything I could to comply. Understandably, rebellion had to be put on standby.

The minute we hit Dover, I'm home. I know it, feel it in my bones, and that's all there is to it! I've got my guitar with me—I'm complete.

We get bused to London then to a plethora of youth hostels along the way to Inverness. It's a five-week trip, so plenty of time to get acquainted with everyone on the bus as well as the fine people of the United Kingdom.

While the boys keep to themselves, I immediately find solace in befriending a member of the other sex, a gorgeous specimen with long brown hair, sensuous lips, and inviting breasts. She's obviously fascinated by the guitar, but I soon discover there's more to it when her tongue finds its way inside my mouth. I deem the Goddess unfazed by what had fazed others before her; reversely, she's wild, fearless, savage... in other words, everything my kind would find desirable in a she-warrior.

We're the first couple to emerge out of the group, and miracle of all miracles, the instructor is willing to look the other way. We're off to a good start!

We kiss for hours on end, our hands wandering between layers to territories in need of charting. There's no doubt passions impede on the best of will to check the scenery outside the bus window, but for now, we're into inner exploring—so may England forgive!

I never knew mouths could hurt from kissing, but they do when overworked. I look with utter fascination at my partner's chapped lips and the redness around them; it's endearing in a special way. It makes me feel like kissing her more, but I refrain. I'm thankful for the privacy offered by high recliners and fleece covers, even if all they provide amounts to an illusion. But I'm far from caring from inside our golden bubble. I forget there's a world outside and life is all the better for it.

A change occurs when crossing into Scotland, as if transitioning into a subtle variance of reality—everything's the same, yet nothing is. We stay in an old, quaint hostel looking toward the ruins of an abbey. There are woods and meadows—a lovers' Eden by all standards. When I claim England's home, I'm actually wrong; rather, the UK's home. And home it is in glorious Scotland, a Goddess by my side as beautiful as she's affectionate! For the very first time, I'm in love with life!

There's much to say about the summer of 1970 in the UK, but nothing ever as strong as the certainty that, one day, I will make it my home. A feeling all the more potent when backed by the vision that I once allegorically crash-landed to my death there, only to be reborn elsewhere. The indelible mark of spatial memory cannot lie. The fingers of synchronicity reach into many hidden places, some perhaps forbidden, and it comes at no surprise that they would also tap into the heart of a very special being, one that can never leave Britain.

It's the end of the trip. My partner and I kiss goodbye. We don't say it, but we know deep down that we shall never see each other again.

With senior high, rises a new sun. Hopes mate with novelty, ambitions swell visionary hearts, hormones fly in hives... I amble in the courtyard, my head full of Britain, out of place, unable to comprehend why I was picked for economics when I chose biochemistry—a subject I'm actually good at. Once again, everything points to an irremediable karmic error. It's hard to not pit all the rights of my recent trip against all the wrongs of before and after it. It's not like I can return the dreaded life and ask for a refund—it's oh so downright sinister!

So, what kind of fuckery am I to expect this time? Should I plan for a surprise, or is it going to be slow and incrementally painful?!

At least, I'm not going to be harassed; I've never met a bully that didn't turn around. I probably will never know what it is that they see, but I don't care one way or the other.

Right off the bat, I home on two Goddesses, a blonde of remarkable beauty, and a petite brunette with a sparkle in her eye, who as irony goes, is in the biochemistry class. All the girls in economics are nondescript brainiacs without an ounce of sexuality. At least, I won't be distracted during class.

The school's in the big city. It's a train ride from home, so all the action happens beyond the parents' line of sight. It's a distinction that translates into more freedom to do all the forbidden things, such as jumping class to play pinball, or hitting the overwhelming goodness of record stores by holing up inside listening booths with piles of new LPs.

I loathe economics, an unbalanced system made to look perfect with a few logical fallacies. Hey, people, workers aren't units whose lives can be manipulated to neatly fit into charts and profit metrics—same with consumers! I barely squeak by the grades. I'm mostly seen with my guitar, swapping licks with kindred souls, endeavoring to learn the entire *Abbey Road* for a show down the line.

Meanwhile, nothing comes of the blonde or the brunette. Both appear to spring from social classes whose concerns eclipse blue collar reality—definitely an issue.

Frankly, I'm somewhat befuddled by my lack of education when it comes to the reality of interacting with higher social castes. It's always been a given that the rich bleeds the poor, but always from a distance, almost like something that exists only for the sake of finding something to complain about, without ever doing anything about it. Now I'm facing the real challenge of breaking through the layers. The revelation is a spear through my heart. I'm awakening to the meaning of social injustice via the channels of impossible romance. But never mind injustice; the point's to break barriers, not in creating new ones. As far as I know, the girls haven't done a thing to send my ship ashore. My parents have for sure, but it's still my ship and I'm on a rectification course!

I'm becoming self-conscious of the sound of my thoughts, to the point of wondering who's doing the talking. I'm full of bravado on the high of a good summer, but I know I must refrain. It's not really me jumping classes, cutting my own throat in the process, or is it? Rebellion isn't me, rebellion is pressure relief activated by the valve of self-preservation, as to not explode or implode. It's the trickle that prevents sanity from collapsing from within. But it's not me. I can't associate with it, anymore than I can associate with the idea that I am doomed to fail because of a cosmic mishap. Rebellion doesn't make me a rebel, it makes me a fool. It's all in my head. I am what I believe I am. If I don't like what I've become; it's time to rethink the process.

Of course, I can't remake the parents or teach them how to remake themselves. It's still a long way up to redemption.

I think all the years of abuse have messed with my mind to the point of distorting my sense of perception of the self. If one minute something makes sense, the next it's its opposite that takes over. The waste of rebellion becomes the only way, and vise versa, in a never-ending rollercoaster. I know that to gain the favors of the blonde, I've got to distinguish myself as a smart, engaging dude, but what do I do instead? I parade grotesqueness like a puppet on drugs; I glorify mediocrity with the illusion of grandeur often associated with repression and fear. I lionize insecurity in a ridiculous display of false bravado bordering on suicide. It's nothing but pure self-loathing on a collision course. It barely amuses the blonde. What an idiot! Unfortunately, that speeding engine has no brakes.

Picking up the pieces is the real work; it's damage control. I rely on the short memory of my student kin, plus a quick attitude adjustment, to sneak out of the image I've made of myself. Let's just pretend it never happened! Surprisingly, it works. For a time. Until the clouds come charging in. Until it's all the same again. Until the blonde and the petite brunette, and all the other players get tired of my shenanigans. I'm a communist, I'm a Nazi, I'm a scholar, I'm a wild guitar player, I'm a hero, I'm an idiot... I don't know who or what I am, and that's the honest truth. I'm looking for an identity, a spine, a foundation to build on... All I have for now is clay crumbling below my lower legs, and maybe a rope tied to a dream without a name. I realize I never had a chance at dating the blonde, or if I did, I miserably blew it. I also come to face that more than a date is blown—the grades are too. I'm flunking economics and the parents are gonna make me pay for it.

The school, in a rare act of generosity, offers to move me to *freighting*, a new trade branch that promises a solid future in job placement and remuneration. (What happened to biochemistry, fuckers!?) It's added pain to injury, another twist of the knife of the ridicule. Can't they just stop with the mental torture already!?

The parents like the option, oblivious of the fact that the only other is me being kicked out of school.

Perception likes to play on the theme of irony.

But before I metaphorically say goodbye to the blonde and the brunette, a Goddess comes my way on my last few days of school. She appears from nowhere as if sent by angels. Man, do we have a good time! When the director caught us, he turned around, red in the face from embarrassment. We have no shame! She loves my long hair and my wild guitar antics—I'm not like the others. She actually digs the rebel in me. She must be a blue collar gal, but I don't bother to ask.

Two days later she's gone and I'm back home—ouch!

Just when I think the hair question is way past us, Father and I, it comes around again with renewed vigor. Out of the blue, the man finds offense with the issue of length, on the premise that the *committee of neighborhood patriarchy* is putting pressure on him to take the wild out of me. In other words he looks weak to the eyes of other men, and God forbids that Father should be seen as a weakling! I don't buy his wrap and for it, I take the beating of my life. He pounds me, pulps me; the devil in him drives him to seeking my death. I retreat to my private cocoon, feeling nothing. When pain no longer has meaning, pain goes—the body simply stops sending signals to the brain, knowing the brain can no longer do anything about its survival. But I survive.

Put simply, the line is crossed. Mother's husband's lost a son. There's no fixing to it. No apologies will ever chisel at the sacredness of that fundamental decision. He never was a father to me—he was merely the hand of tyranny.

I pick up a summer job at a linen cleaning plant. It's terrible work on a lousy early morning schedule and a pittance for wages.

I reconnect with my latest date, but she sees the defeat in me. I'm not the same wild guitar player on a rebellious kick that she knew—the fist of rage took that out of me. She doesn't like what she sees—we part not even as friends.

My father's blows took me back to the middle ages of psychological development, to a critical stage of immaturity caused by the death of the previous ego, forcing the birth of another. As a result, I bear the weight of massive insecurities. As if on cue, the existential panic that had made my life so miserable, years ago, brutally reemerges.

Life, in all its perceivable forms, becomes a nightmare of epic proportions. The world barely exists on the teetering edge of mental and physical ruin. There's no word, no syntactical formation, no language capable of touching the nature of descending into madness. Only those who have known its shores and survived can attest to the damage. There's no sleep, no waking time, no space that isn't affected by the nefarious quality of having one's brain chemistry poisoned by the blackness of an incommensurable evil. If there's a point when nothing matters more than getting to the bottom of the meaning of life, it is *then*, in that all-encompassing vileness. From there, it's nothing but a steep climb up the slippery slope to the high ridge of sanity.

6 – ONE DOWN, ONE UP

If I loathed economics, I can't bother giving the light of day to freighting. It's a disgrace to the creative soul. Who gives a fuck about bills of lading and terms like "merchandising"?! I'm looking for English poetry, not marketing jargon. So, yes, it costs more to ship by plane than it does by truck than it does by train than it does by boat... Who cares?!

That's were I stand with academia. What I know in terms of awareness isn't taught in schools. Life's lessons aren't learned in grammar class, nor are they the sum of numbers. Academic knowledge is the compound lot of things that either get remembered or forgotten for the sake of fitting, or not, within predetermined social classifications. But it's not as much about the knowledge as it is about its distribution. Some get what they want while others pick up the crumbs. I ask for biochemistry, I get economics. How is that for rationale?

I'm caught in between inner crisis and external absurdity, so imagine the joy when I discover that hard liquor can take care of both. A royal knockout!

Of course, I can't afford the cost of bourbon or rum, so some skills not taught in school come in handy. It's a test of confidence: one walks into a liquor store, grabs a bottle, and walks out without raising suspicion. It's fluidity at work, a special dance. The key is to never do the same floor twice in a row, which isn't an issue with so much booze in town. The one problem with liquor is that it can knock me down pretty quick. It takes practice to keep on walking straight, but I hate to say that in spite of my best efforts, I end up doing the stupidest of things, such as throwing typewriters out of windows, or stealing shit I don't need. The worst part is that without knowing it, I'm slowly committing suicide.

One of my buddies and I have gone AWOL. We're in Marseille on our way to Corsica with the cops on our tails. We got busted in a motorcycle shop upon returning to the crime scene after having stolen the carburetor from a Laverda engine and a bunch of leather gear. We flew, but we got traced back to the school at which we were supposed to be studying. We were drunk, of course, which explained the absurdity of the misdeed.

We're insouciantly walking along the old port when a cop van comes to a screeching halt across the promenade, letting out a hostile, yelping bunch of truncheon-wielding agents with all the appearance of coming our way. My friend bolts—a reflex that costs us the charm of innocence. It doesn't take long before we're pinned to the ground and hauled away to one of the city jails. Cause of the arrest: long hair. Reason for prolonged detainment: see top of previous paragraph.

We're transferred back to the north-east where various figures await us at the station, among them, the folks. The person that went by the name of Father barely looks my way, as in being confronted by the ill-product of his work. Mother's mute, ghostly, fixated on my person in ways reminiscent of one attending a funeral, looking one last time at the casket being hoisted down its resting hole. Godmother and her husband are there too, acting the buffer they've acted so many times before. It's a silent ride home full of open wounds and unanswered questions.

Two days later, I down a bottle of scotch with port chasers. I enter a coma.

While a part of me spirals down, another keeps afloat by staying educated. Since freighting isn't gaining traction, I decide to pursue my biochemistry studies in private. The spiraling self steals the books while the one standing near the edge gets to change the course of fate. That's what it looks like from the observer's standpoint.

Debauchery has its pluses—some of the girls are into it. It ain't a lonely world being fucked up half the time. And since I play a mean guitar, I can't complain about the fringe benefits.

The parents don't heed my change in behavior. There's no surprise there, since they've distanced themselves from me; apparently no longer giving a shit about who's failed whom. Whatever money I make on the side, I give to them, like buying my way out of the deal. Twas fun and all—thank you folks!

The failed studies no longer matter. I'm dreaming of big amps and Gibson Les Pauls. I need a job. I'm gonna flunk the finals anyway, so why even show up? I apply for a summer post at the local mill, just to tie me over until I find something more fitting. The weird thing is that the application comes with an aptitude test—another classroom, what the fuck! After that, it's just a waiting game.

Hundreds apply for temp jobs every year, so chances are slim.

I get a note in the mail asking me to show up for an interview. A man in his forties greets me.

"Are you looking for a fulltime position?"
(An odd question since I applied for a temp job.)
"Yes," I lie, sensing trickery.
"Well, congratulations, we need a chemist at the lab, and your test indicates you're familiar with lab work. Would you be OK starting next Monday?"

What about that!?

I thank him, promising I'll be there.

So, fuck freighting, I'll be at the lab during the exam. After all, metallurgical chemistry is only "marginally" removed from biochemistry!

I sense a breath of poetic justice breezing my way.

Kind of a weird déja vu: my record collection friend from way back, also the lead guitarist in our present band while I carry the bass, once handed me the

Beatles' *White Album*, telling me that since he got another copy as a gift, I could keep that one. A month later, he asked for the disks back.

"You gave it to me, pal!"
"No, I didn't!"
"Right, OK, my mistake!"

Sometimes, consciousness takes off on a slant; one never knows...

So, this time around, he borrows my *Live in Tokyo* album by Deep Purple. A month later I ask if he could return it.

"You gave it to me, mate!"
"No, I didn't!"
"Yes, you did!"
"OK, fine, it's yours then!"

I keep my doubts to myself, even when they aren't. I swear I'm not inventing this shit!

The new band's called Rainbow. We're onto something—rock opera et al. We rehearse in this wonderful space up a hill, away from town, next to a mostly vacant football field. The photographer is taking shots of me and the mates—we're the real thing and we feel quite good about ourselves. The gigs that follow are well received and reviewed, but (the dreadful "but" again) egos being egos, they seem to find a way to mess things up, and it takes no time for the band to fall apart. Still, a minor success is a giant step that somehow puts my name on the list of visible players. Other bands are formed, all doomed to short life cycles, and so it goes for a while. I now own a Fender Telecaster and a Super Reverb; not quite the Les Paul and Hiwatt, but I'm saving.

At last, I'm free from the parents, but the work hours are gruesome, especially the morning shift. The job also interferes with my musical lifestyle, forcing me to consider the options. There's also the sense that I have betrayed my private ambitions of becoming a scholar. Deep inside, in spite of my aversion to the academic system, I consider that knowledge provides a true platform to respectability. In some way, emotional release via the foolishness of rebellion did nothing but nil my chances at building a dignified character. The remaining option is to keep on studying for a degree in chemistry. Just to balance the act, I also join the conservatory of music for the last course available: upright bass. Hello Bartók! Coincidentally, the school's director is the old man of the blonde from a couple of years back. What goes around comes around. But do I have a chance at breaking the class barrier? Perhaps, but not with the army knocking at the door!

I have time—my turn's a year down the road. Surely, there's a way to go around the problem, like bailing out of the old country for some new world. Britain's always the first choice, and I'm gearing up for a one-way ticket. There's also the offer of joining a commune in Mérida, Venezuela, on a plantation owned by the parents of a U.S. friend. My sense of adventure pushes for it.

One may say life's full of speed bumps, some more useful than others. One of them is yet another Goddess, who, in layman's terms, belongs to the drummer. Loyalties stand no chance to hormones, and neither does sanity. For the sake of an unattainable romance, I procrastinate with my one option at skipping the army, allowing my life to come too close to its vortex. Suction is inevitable—it arrives in the form of an official mail that demands I show up for the preliminary exams scheduled a short distance down the line. Panic strikes without mercy; my compass's directionless—I'm a cornered animal.

What's left is to go with the flow in hopes of a miracle. There's no way I'm psychologically fit for combat. It's not that I don't believe in war; it's all over the map! It's that I don't believe the basis for war is justified. For those who've paid attention to history class, you know just as well as I do that all wars play on the same theme: the pathology of power and greed—the plague of rule, aft and fro the ages.

I'm off to the exams. Fate-shaping will dictate the course to follow.

Fate-shaping isn't boding well. The MDs and the psychologists are motherfuckers cut out from an army template. Anyone aware of the work of Nazi doctors in the last war, would home on a resemblance with these guys—hard, inexorable, and desensitized. I miserably fail at persuading them that my hypersensitivity to the industrial military complex is grounds for an exemption. I'm physically sound, thus deemed the perfect material to be joining the ranks of combatants. Of course, heavily leaning on a psychological profile bent on depravity comes short of impressing the pros at detecting poorly rehearsed acts. It's worth the shot, but it falls flat on its face.

I've got three months to get out of Dodge—the obstacles are many.

Nothing much can stand to raging hormones—the proof lies in my inability to let go of the drummer's girlfriend. Short of fucking, we've got a lot of ground covered. It's too much of an investment—I surrender to the flesh.

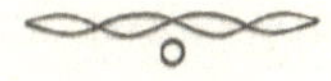

7 – TROUBLED SKIES

The one thing I don't do is fake ignorance. My score for the army's written test is one-ninety-eight out of two-hundred; something rarely heard of in those circles.

The one thing I do, on the other hand, is make rash, irrational decisions. Just to prove that stupidity and knowledge can become easy bedfellows.

When informed that the option to join the elite group of Officer Cadets is open to me, I write back telling the army to fuck off. Just like that, I get to swap a relatively pleasant year as a respected temporary officer, with the hell of a mine detector operator, aka the first man to die in battle.

The first day promises. An idiot pulls some of my hair off while screaming some nonsense an inch away from my face. I don't doubt he's full of raging testosterones. I smell trouble for freedom.

I don't know what makes me do it, but before we're due to swap our civilian clothes for the army garb, I pack a bundle of my threads and stash it in a bush outside the dormitory. I don't question instincts when they surge; it's part of survival.

It doesn't take me long to discover that the army is Hell on Earth. Nothing compares to it, except for some versions of familial reality. But I'm no longer in a closed unit of abuse; this is the outside, albeit a container inside the outside. OK, I get it; I should have bailed when I could have. An idea that proves contagious.

In spite of my objections, four men grab me, tie me to a chair, and shave my noggin. I see red, as a nosy bunch laugh their heads off. After the deed, I'm sent off with all the confidence of a shorn sheep. Nothing about it sits well with me; I'm boiling inside, plotting my next move. Always trust your instincts; thus the emergency pack hidden in the bushes.

It's eleven, or twenty-three—whatever—an hour past the final inspection. My guitar and I, plus one of the guys—a convict on civic duty—ease our way out through the dorm window and land in the grass outside. I don't presume anyone sees us. I reconnect with my gear: jeans, bomber jacket, papers et al, then the mate and I endeavor to jump over the security wall, behind the back of the guards on duty.

The night sky is full of stars, a sign of promise. My papers are in order, but I have to lose the convict before the border. Not only will he not make it, but he's bound to compromise me. What took me to encumber myself with his presence? He kinda volunteered at a time when my thinking was busy with private reality. In other words, I inherited a dead weight out of the goodwill of distraction.

A rare car speeds by us as we hit the ditch. We walk a lonely country road lined on one side by the deep, near-motionless river, and on the other, by fenced pastures and orchards. All radiates under the light of a glorious full moon.

It's dawn when we arrive at the border. I ask the mate to keep his distance so that I can cross first. The customs agent is a fat, fortyish man with a red, piggish face, whose hazed-over eyes can't decide whether to focus on my face or the passport picture. Factoring in the relative latency of his hangovered brain, it's no surprise it takes him so long to get going. The action consists of a guttural grunt followed by two men flanking me with the aim of preventing me from bolting, which I have no intention of doing since I'm technically legit.

Something's wrong.

I say "technically" because there's an unforeseen clause in any unscheduled departure from the army; it goes: *Snitches and Cowards are at Liberty to Report on all Deviant Acts.*

"I don't presume anyone sees us," is the assumption that leaves the main box unchecked—the one that says, *Make Sure No-one sees you!*

So, the military police has been on me from the get-go. All they had to do was spread the news and wait for someone to call. How resourceful! Just when I thought I had all the time in the world to get my ass out of harm's way, I'm instead being hauled away from the border jail to the justice system of men in uniform.

It turns out that in the history of this particular regiment, no-one has ever gone AWOL on their first day. The rare distinction merits a ninety day sentence. Pending behavioral report, that amount's open to a spectrum of pluses and minuses. Whatever the case, the silver lining keeps me out of the loop of duty and senseless training.

It goes without saying that my civilian clothes and guitar get impounded until further notice. A gleeful look points in the direction of indefiniteness. That sucks!

I'm barely two weeks in the hole when a benevolent soul fetches me to introduce me to my new job. There must be an angel somewhere because I find myself in charge of dispatching fresh laundry from behind the Dutch door of a third floor facility inclusive of private digs. Plus I'm put in charge of the keys to the storage of all things civilian, coincidentally getting me reunited with my guitar and the rest of my stuff, which I arrange to conceal once and for all.

My past is so full of irony, that my educated taste for the irony of the present is savored in measured doses. From up under the rafters, I watch the progress of my mates struggling under the weight of barked orders, while in the back of my sheltered room, the radio plays *Reelin' In the Years*.

As days pass, I settle in the numbing routine of the predictable. My hair grows beyond the approved threshold, but since none of the officers make it to laundry dispatch, it doesn't matter. Rather than joining for the meals, I get my food straight from the kitchen, courtesy sympathetic souls and forgotten doors. In fact, I'm just as forgotten as the doors I traverse, my identity lost amidst the shelves and chutes of room 315, on the third floor of building four. Invisibility lies in the refined particulars of exposure.

I'm three months in and I haven't seen a gun. I now wear U.S. army khakis found deep down the strata of garb history, something that in spite of all reasons to not exist, found a unique way to go around the improbability of being worn again. I've been thinking that normality is life's most alien component.

I'm putting much practice into the guitar, which contradicts what I was told before being drafted. But then again, this isn't a regular situation. In fact, it's just as unusual as me wearing U.S. army threads.

Something breaks through the layers at the speed of light. As I walk my regular route back from the kitchen, an order comes barking my way, demanding that I explain my disheveled presence on the base. The veil of invisibility is yanked by the malevolent hand of bad timing. A somnolent form of arrogance has barred me from heeding the stillness of complacency. Or maybe arrogance and complacency are interchangeable here— the thing is I'm royally fucked!

My new job is to scrub the latrines and the tiled floors with a toothbrush, which is the bad news. The good news is that my guitar and civilian clothes are safe in a secret hideaway.

My exposure to the outside world comes with fresh acquaintances. I'm inexorably drawn to the troublemakers, the unfixable rebels, or those with plans that run counterclockwise to the system, such as the hardcore left-wingers.

My association with politics is chaotic and directionless. My stand as a dissatisfied member of society might deserve the dreaded communist moniker, but frankly, I couldn't care less. Call me an anarchist if you wish!

A hard-boiled mate assisting with the furnaces connects me with a private shower. The idea of a bunch of naked lads put together in one room simply doesn't agree with me. The psychology is nonexistent; it's just a matter of preference. I like to do my thinking under the jet, as uncomplicated as that!

The mate in question is an unbreakable sort. He simply doesn't give a shit about the barking outside him. He's smarter than all of them put together and makes a point of it with unrestrained impunity. A mix of scorn and pity is his weapon of choice. I take notes. He's the one who tells me to not get mixed in with politics—it goes nowhere in his book.

If politics doesn't rotate my world, injustice does. And injustice is the proud motto of the ground forces— the more the better. According to them, without them saying it, bending to injustice is the stuff that turns boys into men. The hard love of men abusing men is good for ya, according to the unwritten clauses of army rationale. To me, it's nothing more than a myth rooted in the tyranny of history.

It turns out that left-wing politics feed on the semantics of injustice. They have good reasons for it, explained in terms of irrefutable power. The senior mate, who endeavors to like me, is a teacher of far-left rhetorics; also a young professor when he's not wasting his time in the army. He's charismatic and affectionable in his doe-eyed kind of way. He's probably a fanatic, but I find him inoffensive. I feel safe with him. Although he's only eight years older than I am, he radiates a patriarchal substance that adds glue to our relationship. I'm warned by the furnace guy, but I heed not the message.

Said furnace friend introduces me to science-fiction—works by Philip K. Dick, Ray Bradbury, Jack Williamson... "It's all the politics you need, mate!" he states, sounding the inevitability of facts.

My normal reading revolves around science, mainly, the biology of the human body. But, ironically, there's a line that ties fantasy to the far from unfantastic world of experimental science. Take alien probing, for instance... I come to realize that sci-fi is the vision of the future brought to us on a reversed temporal template, each story a window into dynamic foreseeability.

Does sci-fi add to the meaning of life? Not any more than science does. To the contrary, science takes me further and further away from any meaning relevant to purpose. Deep fiction, on the other hand, let's me contemplate possibilities in quasi-infinite variations.

For life to gain meaning though, it will have to take a hell of a lot more than science or fringe literature. On the one hand, I don't need educated deciphering of the things I can see, touch, hear, and smell; on the other, wandering aimlessly into possibilities emergent of other's visions is hardly a personal quest.

Action takes my mind away from circular thinking. The prof and I meet with sympathetic aliens in the backrooms of universities to discuss the logistics of inflicting ruin on the occupying forces. It's invigorating in ways that bring elements of purpose to my life, something that besides music has been lacking for, well, ever.

Insiders are required, which makes two of us. It's evident we're working for a foreign group with foreign agendas and concerns. We're aware of the consequences, but who doesn't fancy the occasional dare in an otherwise bleak existence? We just have to watch our backs in novel ways.

The nicest thing for me is mobility. My civilian clothes and multi-lingual abilities provide the necessary means to exist incognito among the natives. Naturally, I can't go out through the base's main gate; hence the must for choreographed exits and reentries over the wall.

Even the most difficult of tasks become instinctual after a while. Predictable patterns, inclusive of the rare unpredictability, are easily covered with practice.

There's no need to talk about whatever the army throws at me—it's never going to be nice. Just to sum it up, I shoot guns at targets and go on long foot-bleeding marches, carrying various weighty contraptions. It's a lead cross, garnering inertia with each step. Enough said!

My pal from the furnace is finally released from duty, a whole half-year past his original scheduled exit, all that because of the time he spent in jail for insubordination. Got to admire the dude!

I visit him in the capital on one of my illegal sorties. I like his lifestyle, which involves copious amounts of hash and acid.

The aliens' callous plan is for us to take control of the base, armory et al. Recruiting is essential, requiring trust and stealth. The proposition seems to attract more criminal minds than true cause-fighters, a detail the prof is impervious to. I vacillate between going forward and calling the game off. There's enough insanity to the method for my own to question the soundness of the planned operation. But I'm too deep in and fortitude is at stake, so I forge ahead. I'm not totally blind to the suicidal side of going forward with it—there's little doubt the authorities will use force to tame the insurrection.

Out of the blue, the whole thing rings hollow. I equate it to the unrealism of building something out of nothing; like when I was a kid intent on building a bicycle out of old rubber treads and a few sticks. Conceptual logic isn't the same as the concretization of a robust scheme. The thought stems from my lack of trust in the recruits. It's unlikely they'll go through it. They want us to go ahead, but I think it's mostly because they're bored and need excitement. At the first shot, they'll be running like rabbits. But the prof remains unconvinced—he's sure it will work.

Well, the prof is wrong. We're whisked to the interrogation room merely a day before the start of the mutiny. It's highly probable that one of the team was a mole, feeding the cops everything they asked for.

As it turns out, one of the team was a mole!

While the interrogators beat the crap out of the weakest elements to get them to talk, they're careful with me and the prof. The babble of the weak stands no chance against the silence of the strong. What they know is unsubstantial; it might as well be a framing job by a witless character, someone challenged by education. They get nothing out of us except requests for lawyers, to which they claim we're not entitled to a defense, but we know better. It's a game of wasted weeks getting nowhere, while they go on a loop of deep search of our belongings.

Then, one day, the prof is gone, sent to another regiment across the land. I learn it from a note he manages to squeak by the guards. He's victorious in his defeat, but that's the prof for you—I knew he was a fanatic—fanatics never lose; they die martyrs.

That leaves me to deal—alone—with military intelligence (an oxymoron), which now has ammo in the form of the prof's pseudo-culpability. Somehow, the lie makes them think they no longer need to abide to the civilian code of ethics. But in spite of what they think about me, I'm vulnerable. I'm not as much worried as weary. They're testing my limits and I'm getting tired of feeding them what they want to hear while actually giving nothing away; and they're getting tired too, and desperate.

The whole charade stops cold when one of the noses pulls out, from of the inner jacket of the *Duane Allman Anthology*, a copy of a letter to the First Minister, denouncing, in order of importance, the army's abject disregard to protocol and its related items of corruption.

I have no idea why I still have one of those lying around, but it's beyond the point—I'm fucked!

There's no tribunal, no defense—forget verdicts—the punishment for treason is five years in maximum-security military jail, aka the fortress.

But something backfires. Not only do the aliens picket outside the base—an act unparalleled in the annals of international tensions—but copies of the very letter that got me busted is sent to all major papers and lawyers, resulting in the buildup of a crackerjack defense team eager to take on the shenanigans of the armed forces. Just like that, I no longer qualify for the dungeon. No case and no charges ever existed, and I'm free to roam the base to my liking.

But never underestimate the army; it's a bedrock institution as old as religion, whose old tricks constantly reinvent themselves. One may shake its foundation, but its edifice is built to stand the test of time.

Free to roam is a figure of speech. A rowdy party with fresh-from-battle ally forces puts me in a jeopardized position vis à vis protocol. That's all it takes to get the gears to mesh. "No mixing with the Americans!" they order. I disagree—I mix with the Americans, make friends with the Americans, drink their beer, hear their stories. They are better soldiers—braver men.

There are no guidelines, no methodology when it comes to soldiers like me or my furnace friend. I'm hard to pin down. I'm the sweet and sour to the army's meat and potatoes. I'm a sore that needs removal.

I'm thrown into a subterranean cell with no light but the jaundice glow of a weak incandescent bulb. The shitter's at the end of a tapered tunnel, consisting of a hole in the concrete floor, stinking of something that has stunk for too long. Intuition tells me that Death herself was seen visiting the place—I can feel her mark in its ravaged spatial geometry. People have died here. It occurs to me the space doesn't exist—never has. Whoever goes in is never seen again...

A kindred soul leaves a bottle of scotch on my side of the rusty bars. The alcohol cuts the cold that sticks to my bones, covers the smell of black mold that lives everywhere, on the walls, the ceilings, within the fibers of the damp mattress and covers—the mold that relentlessly deposits its spores on my skin and inside my lungs. But the drinking makes me sick, even in small amounts. I crawl to the hole at the end of the tunnel to puke booze and blood. I feel like staying there, at the end of my journey. I think of my guitar, safe where it is stashed.

I get a visit from one of the officers, whose face shows the stigma of alarm. He's not like the others. He cares. He arranges to have me transferred to a military hospital a ways away from slow death, but unbeknownst to him, he underestimates the continuity of evil that lives in mycological realism below the surface. The head psychologist, in cahoots with intelligence, I am certain, prescribes a Machiavellian diet of uppers and downers meant to kill a horse, to be administered at hourly intervals. I get it; since death by mold failed, a heart attack is now the demise of choice.

I'm so weary, yet my entire body shakes, unable to rest. I drift in and out of reality like a sickened soul on a rolling sea. The intoxication takes hold of body and mind. I have no wish to live or die—the aperture of consciousness closes to a pinhole. I'm so tired...

Mother...? Is that you, Mother? Yes, yes, I hear you—the electroshock treatment... Nasty buggers, ain't they, the shocks?! You're tired too; I understand—no rest for the wicked though—but you mustn't sleep or they will take your vitals away; you know what for, don't ya? Well, tis nice seeing you again, Mother, ta-ta!

I wake up in the elevator, stuck between the top floor and the roof. They send a crew to get me. The psychologist, a lieutenant colonel, thinks I'm nothing but trouble. He sends me back to base infirmary.

A year and three months have passed since I entered the army. I occasionally jump the wall to ascertain that choice is still one of the few items I possess, with my guitar and some groovy threads, but the excitement is no longer there. I prefer to hole up in the secret space that has been my sanctuary for most of my stay, a forgotten music room only accessed by an obstructed rear entrance in the back of the kitchens. I'm the only one left to know the whereabouts of its skeleton key. The place is where my things are kept, in a closet hidden by boxes. By the old turntable lie *Duane's Anthology*, the Mother's *We're only in it for the Money*, and Steely Dan's *Can't buy a Thrill*, some of the few albums that keep my heart from sinking. I also have my flute, which I never mention. I have no idea why I don't, because it's a fine instrument. I bought it right after hearing *In the Court of the Crimson King* way back when.

I spend the rest of my army time in the infirmary, recuperating from multiple addictions. The cool officer, who got me out of the hole, visits me on and off. Turns out he's a government agent on his way to create much trouble for the army, but I shouldn't say.

In some odd way, I both win and lose, but then again, I never sought battle.

The Colonel signs my release papers and shakes my hand like nothing happened. Instead of meeting my freedom through the main gate, I reconnect with the wall, lower my guitar, throw my bag, and jump to the asphalt.

I light a cigarette, briefly looking around, then decide to hitch a ride to the border.

8 – THE LAST STRAW

Home is no longer home; it's a place to hole up till things get sorted out. The army's behind me; it's a good thing, but I have little energy to reconnect with the lab and resume work. I could use a vacation in a place like Corsica, on a golden beach, with a Black Label and Coke.

Women have been off my radar for a long time, probably because of the bromide in the food at the barracks. Crazy world we live in...

I can barely hold a spoon when I eat—my nerves are shot. I trust I will get better, but I would be lying if I denied being worried about what the drugs did to me. It feels like my ego was murdered again. If memory serves, the current one is my third. One sure way to lose your footing, not to mention your confidence!

I eventually get back to work and reconnect with old friends. I use army money and some savings to purchase a Gibson Les Paul Deluxe, with the intention of putting a new group together—the sooner the better.

But my mind is playing tricks on me, while an existential front looms in the distance.

I visit my old furnace buddy in the capital, who suggests I should get away from my past. He has a point.

I let the concept grow on me, there's no rush, plus a rash move is beyond me at this point.

I don't think there's a more vacuous time than the one I'm living in. Nothing congeals. The lab and the classes carry no message, no hope. There's no future down that road, just a stretch to the final line with no statement made, a bed with a dying corpse full of nostalgia for the unaccomplished.

The old band's lead singer bailed out to England like I should have done before being drafted. He writes saying he works doing sound for Stray, a middle of the road player on the London rock scene. I want to be there, but mental fatigue has fixed me with lead shoes. Instead, I make a habit of frequenting a lonely bar out of the way of acquaintances, of drinking Heineken while the waitress sits on my lap—one of the benefits of being the only patronage. It suits me to exist in my own alienness.

All plays on a slow theme—a forty-five tango spinning at thirty-three on a background of monochromatic ambers under the low pressure sodium of numbness. Straight words are redefined in lose allegories, in unapologetic associations with the vaguely related. It is a time when the meaning of life becomes an obstacle to seeking nothingness, to disappear from the layers of perception—to never have existed.

My poor little brother, who wishes for a big one to admire and get inspired by, is served the cold dish of emotional rejection. I have nothing for him but a picture of mental annihilation that crumbles between his small fingers. I'm no point of reference for a young soul. May the parents do their fucking job and spare him the misery of self-deprecation!

I constantly hear there are answers to everyone's questions. Gurus, for a fee, will show the way. Moonies, for no money, will tell you that guns are necessary evils against the ever-present forces that seek to destroy Moonies. Metaphysical studies promise but can't let go of their spooks. Maybe questions and answers are the wrong way to go about making sense...

Bit by bit, the colors return to the light of day, and with it, the drive to shake things loose. I practice with the drummer, now girlfriendless, in hopes of putting a solid band together. I show up in town; hang out with all the visible musicians, shoot the breeze about gear, dreams, and opportunities. Anyone with decent equipment is a star in his own eyes. I say he, because the shes don't play rock; they just fuck rockers. It's too bad; they should check Fanny out. But no-one knows who Fanny is—only me. Nothing much has changed since before the army, same people, same talks, same unexplored visions... I'm reawakening to the reality of being in the wrong place.

The friend's advice is becoming the mantra that refuses to let go. *Get away from your past!* impregnates my thoughts, steals the space once reserved for excuses, albeit without the means to provide the trigger.

No, the trigger comes from elsewhere; from a place so visible that I have become blind to it: Mother.

Mother hasn't screamed for a while, or rather, I've become impervious to the screaming; but today, the screaming is loud, clear, and nonsensical. It has no root, no aim, no reason to exist, yet it is felt as much as heard. It contains all the past resentments, all the pains, all the history of a soul deprived of childhood, play, love; all the rage of frustration, anguish, and fear of those whose lives have been stolen. It is visceral, vicious, sinister, deadly... I recoil in shock, never imagining a time like this would come, especially now, at a non-conjuncture. There is hatred for humanity in it; a wish to obliterate all of its parts, an evil so great that it's a miracle such a small body is able to contain it. All I can say is, "Fuck off!"

I throw the Les Paul in its case, grab a few clothes, and hit the last train to the main station where I purchase a ticket for London.

The timing isn't right. Unlike my first visit over five years ago, I'm a stranger in a strange land. Since I can't reconnect with the singer, I'm left to shack at a youth hostel by Victoria Station, an old stone building that smells of piss and whose clientele is best described as an in and out of unkempt vagrants. Talk about being out of place!

After a few days of aimless wanderings, I make my way to Paris to seek the mysterious fortune awaiting me there. The old friend offers his casa as a temporary measure against living on the street, but the studio space is small, and as one says, "Visitors are like fish, after three days the place stinks!"

While it's still good, we enjoy the company of the two prostitutes residing next door. Their stories are as funny as they are pathetic—men are depraved, multi-faced pigs, walking caricatures of everything gone wrong with the gene pool. But the gals are strong and used to all kinds of shenanigans, plus they pack heat!

We meet gay prostitutes with whom we bicycle the streets with all the insouciance of the free. We know we're slaves, but nothing can steal the moment—not with such good acid.

Eventually, the fish quote proves true. A slight mounting of tension is the green light to my exit, But a few days is enough time to meet new faces and find refuge; and so, I leave the guitar with a lovely couple and their one year old, promising to return after completion of some urgent business. The truth is that I'm broke and due to collect at the mill back east. Also, I want to fetch my amp which I'm dearly missing. That unavoidably calls for a visit with the old folks—something I'm definitely not looking forward to.

In spite of my unapologetic two-week no-show, the lab is expecting my return to the fold. Before I have a chance to tell the director that I've no intention to resume, he vociferates that it's only out of Christian charity that I'm allowed to reassume my post, and that he has no choice but to lay me off for another week. The guy's unreal! "Fuck Christian charity, Sir; I'm here to collect the money you owe me!"

Once more, I'm off to the capital to join the couple and the baby. Of course, nothing comes for nothing; hence why I'm in charge of the rent and the babysitting. In other words, I pull another short straw out of the same old bag of tricks. But enough is enough; my furnace friend calls the house to inform me that digs are opening in the suburbs and to get my ass over there before the couple bleeds me dry. It's an empty three roomer on the twelfth floor of a tower overlooking other towers being built. I still hear farmland and forest calling from below the mess.

By now I'm so broke that I have to hit commuters for coins to buy the train fare to my new job as an Offset printing machine operator at a downtown insurance company. So far, I'm not finding the silver lining.

Before long, I'm being drawn into schemes with criminals passing as good guys. It's amazing how many of them are out there! As alluring as it might be, the thrill only seeks to reconnect me with the worst of my past, when said past is the last thing I want to relive. But a note from London, forwarded from the old address, arrives just in time. I'm needed there, no excuses allowed!

I cash my last paycheck and clean my account; I don't tell anyone I'm skipping town. It's a vanishing act without a trick. If the ego must die, let it be my choice; I shall be reborn the man I wish I'd become. But instead, the jewel turned to coal, and coal to smoke and ash. As the clock rings the hour, the time is right to die the righteous death.

9 – THE RISE

It's a beautiful day on the channel, with just the right puffy clouds spotting the sky. The waters are calm and welcoming. Seagulls follow the boat—free on their coast to coast flight. I too am free to cross borders; no pig-faced agent to block my way this time around. Rather it's smiles and welcomes, a quick stamp of approval at the gates of a brand new world, or is she an old friend opening her arms? The stranger was the other me after all; the strange land, his obscured vision. It's alright now.

When I arrive at the house, a stunningly beautiful gypsy queen and her biker boyfriend welcome me with the warmth of those who know from mysterious future channels who their friends are. It's called instant bonding, I guess. The singer's late from work, so we make small talk over tea and a joint.

To me, the singer will always be the singer, even though he no longer sings. He never sang that well in the first place, but that's not the point. He's a great friend and that's what counts.

He introduces me to the house band. We jam, I'm in; it's all in the timing. We go out for pints to seal the deal.

'Turns out my fave amp company's just a stone's throw down the road. As it so happens, I'm in the market for bigger wattage—timing again!

Common sense dictates that I find myself a job. The first place I check hires me on the spot. So now, after three days in the new world as a new man, I have a home, a band, and a job. Interestingly, it is a time when jobs, bands, and places to live are hard to find, especially for an alien. But I'm no alien; I just had to make a dumb detour for reasons that may still be tied to the meaning of life...

Now's the time and space for name dropping; but I must refrain. When the timing's right, it's hard to go wrong. Even if one tried to, timing wouldn't allow for it. Let me just say that, from a certain standpoint, I'm a lucky bastard.

Let the chips fall where they may!

As I said, there's hardly anything I can do wrong; even fuckups sounds good to my growing fan base—it's almost embarrassing when they ask for more—but with good timing, the place is always right. It's interesting how the continuum works; I'm no Einstein, but I wake up in the middle of the night thinking about that shit. Without space and time, we're left with dreams, where all places exist as one, and time knows of no past or future. It's a bit like that on a stage too. It's an ambiance rather than the time-related sequence of such and such song starting and ending within precise confines. On stage, time's elastic. It's also elastic when one travels—one being me of course—as it seems it stretches. Weeks become long-weeks and a month, a long-month. As to space, well, it's a matter of perspective, isn't it?

Take someone who's never traveled outside their small valley; the world is what they see, a place rich in details, but short on span. It's a choice—nothing to do with space. I don't know if you're getting what I'm aiming at... Never mind, where was I? Alright, so take the adventurous of mind who climbs the mountain to check out what's beyond, say; does the world become bigger because s/he sees more small valleys tucked in between the next rows of summits, or is it made smaller because what s/he sees is far bigger than what s/he had imagined? One can't tell, right? That's what I mean by elastic—intractable, perceptual evasiveness.

I'm lost in the narrative. Should I keep my thoughts to myself, or share with the imaginary audience that is also the self? A big, ambiguous question that calls for recess.

...

Alright, that was strange. I'm not a big fan of echo chambers when seen from the inside, but I've made my peace: the audience wins! Oh, sweet madness!

The singer, who, as I recently learned, was a gay prostitute in the old country, is now strictly sticking to the company of pubescent boys. I'm not sure I relate, but rock and roll is neither a clean nor ethical place; which isn't the same as saying there's no sanity amid the mayhem. Some of my very visible friends are drugless vegetarians with exemplary family lives; but that's more the exception than the rule. If there's one area that has no appeal to me; it's the rabbit hole of addictions. It's bad enough with alcohol, but smack and speed by injection and mountains of coke is a totally inane road to follow. Sorry, mates, you're totally out of your minds!

That's how I lose the singer. At least he goes to sleep with a smile.

I get in touch with the Maharishi around the time my old drummer, the one with the girlfriend I dug, joins me. We're barely into a month of rehearsal when he takes so much acid that he ends up riding a sled in Siberia.

Within days, he joins the TM Sidhi programme, sells his Hayman kit, and moves to Switzerland.

Damn, the past can't stick to the present!

With the singer and the drummer gone, there's nothing left for me to look back at. The old past has shut its doors, and now I'm free to create a new one.

Transcendental Meditation is alright, but it's nothing more than sitting for twenty minutes twice a day repeating a private mantra that may, or not, be more than one chosen amid a few. All I know is that it doesn't make people better; it just slows their momentum down. What I gain is that it's OK to sit and do nothing. It's not a race out there, it's merely an obstacle course that needs to be negotiated with vigor and precision, and whose only finish line is death. No need to compete as I see it.

But no, meditation doesn't lead to levitation and out of body experiences—not at my end. It's not quite snake oil for the soul, but who am I to say what it is?! Perspective, peeps! Speaking of it, perspective is relative; thus technically neither right nor wrong. It would be like saying that a particular kind of human is right or wrong because of their uniqueness, which could be anything from their tastes in food to their skin color. The thought is kind of appalling. But I'm constantly amazed by uneducated opinions, which I must iterate, have nothing to do with being any sort of human. Opinions are intellectual constructs borne of the synthesis of multiple beliefs formed into a system. But then rises the paradox: if opinions aren't to define right and wrong, what makes them different from perspectives which are neither right nor wrong? As I said, it's the kind of shit that wakes me up in the middle of the night.

I like my American girlfriend. She came for an audition and won my heart. But the band can't care less for her—she's no Janis, more like a Joni—so now we deal with tensions. We cut a few demos with her, but I can't convince a bunch of chauvinistic egos to become better men—they can't help showing their discontent. Problem is, they can't afford to lose me, because technically, I'm the bandleader.

The rhythm guitarist and I get invited to jam with a legend. My girlfriend isn't invited, but she comes all the same. I don't really want her there, but "legend" is the keyword that green-lights forcefulness. For the first time, she really pisses me off. It's also a good excuse for the bandmate to unleash some nasty misogynistic one-liners in her direction. For once, I don't care!

Shit goes down. I have this huge argument with said girlfriend that leads to her being banned out of the jam. I'm hurt and angry. My recourse to using a term that cuts the relationship in half is irreversible. Another fork in the road—some is gained, some is lost.

So, instead of getting married in the U.S., I'm single in the UK. There's a ring for a song to it that I might explore when my brain chemistry recovers from the shock. A heartbreak's always a heartbreak.

In the meantime there's a rock opera in the making on which I share guitar duty with the legend. So, in spite of the breakup, England has delivered on her promise.

With the female singer gone, the lads get all worked up about getting male pipes with brass balls, but I'm not sure that's the way I want to go. I'm not here to carry over past resentments into a display of male solidarity—I'm looking for authenticity regardless of the form, save for punk, which I've grown too old for, but it gets my respect all the same. May the youth forge ahead!

All this to say it's time to move on and bid the band a fond farewell!

The opera is a resounding success. Of course, I'm only one of the many musicians on the double album, but what a list! It's enough for me to get a head start into exploring options, musical and not, and to put a down payment on a house in Camden Town. Not the most fashionable of places, but I smell a change of winds in the real estate market. The idea for the house is to build a 24 track recording studio in it. It's big enough and the walled yard is a plus for privacy. For the time being, the area consists of a lot of vacant council housing rife with squatters, but I'm hopeful. I'm also eyeing a place in the country where the legend and his friends live—some of them even bigger legends. At any rate, people are people—I'm just glad to be reunited with my family of consciousness.

Between the TM and the vegetarian diet, I live a pretty clean life. I've even quit tobacco; a much bigger bitch to drop than anticipated. So, with just the occasional pint, I'm pretty much a saint, which allows me the vantage point of observing carnage among my kin. Not that I'm much interested in the psychology of fame and fast in-and-out monies, but it's unavoidable, especially with a clear mind. To this point, I don't understand why one would obliterate their present for the purpose of rejoicing about it. Isn't the celebratory pint enough of a symbolic accent? I would think of better ways to enjoy the cosmic gift of professional success besides yard-long lines of coke.

Before becoming a saint, I too ventured that lane. I think the last time was when a producer mate of mine and I found ourselves in the middle of a field, inside a Benz convertible, in our pajamas, without any recollection of how we got there. It was on a fine Sunday morning and the first thing that came to our minds was to open the village pub at nine o'clock, which the ownership obliged, because you know—"legends." If you can imagine grownup kids on a rampage; that was us! By the time the hordes came in, the producer announced that I was purchasing his house, a mansion up the side of a hill with a natural stream running through its living room, its grounds overlooking the round tower of a famous recording studio. No doubt it was a nice place, but I had no memory of having made such a deal. Nonetheless, the party went on until the producer passed out in the middle of a public announcement. He fell flat on his back, his face the grey of death. When the paramedics arrived to haul him away, he sprung up, raised his glass, and declared, "You men are true professionals!"

That was the cut-off point for me. One doesn't play with the honorable and the dignified like they're merely there for the amusement of the drunken rich. I felt utterly embarrassed in my own drunkenness. The game was aimless. It wasn't even a game.

I hear that Father passed. "Good riddance!" is the first thought that crosses my mind. Not the nicest thing to come up with, I gather; but now isn't the time for forgiveness. I also hear that in his last years, he took on to painting and became locally famous for his unique take on the naïve genre. Who would have thought!

I barely wonder how Mother's doing—I'm sure she's going to put on the mourning act—but I know that, deep inside, she's probably relieved.

I stay in touch with my sisters whom I've always adored in spite of me having once called them useless—but it wasn't their fault. The biological family exists behind the fog of memory, memories that belong to another me, but reality being what it is, even if the past can somewhat be reshaped, they stick around, feeble as they may be. Although, I'm glad my sisters are very much present.

The legend asks me to come to New York with him. He wants to introduce me to some of his friends, whom he calls the family; a term he picked up from me in reference to families of consciousness. No, nothing that pertains to TM! As a matter of fact, I'm done with the Maharishi—I came to realize I don't fit the profile anymore—nothing personal.

While in Manhattan, I connect with my ex-girlfriend, who lives on Long Island quite a way in. I suggest she meets me at my hotel, but she instead invites me to her parents' house. I've had my share of bad ideas in my life and that one sounds really bad; plus it's a two-hour train ride. I only want to hear about how her singing's doing—nothing more—she deserves a break. I give her a couple of names and numbers, wishing her good luck.

One of the family members just lost his lead guitarist, so we jam with a couple of the boys from Jersey. He once had a number one hit, but I think his newer material could need a lift and I have ideas. That's not what he's looking for though—he just wants me to play my Les Paul like the hero whom I'm supposed to cover for. It just doesn't feel right—maybe another time—nothing gained, nothing lost.

"Legend" is starting to feel a tad equivocal, so it's El Jay from now on. So, while El Jay takes off for L.A., I ponder on the possibilities. New York isn't a bad place when you know the right people, but it feels somewhat affected and self-conscious. I have a sense that one needs to be born here to get the gist of what NY's all about. I can't quite focus, even my vision is blurred. Most of the people I meet are ungrounded, flighty to the point of hollow, or phony, as they say here. I've never been around anyone asking a question, and then leaving without waiting for an answer—it's frankly insulting! And here, it seems to be the social norm. I don't think I can get used to it.

In all fairness, not all New Yorkers are afflicted with short attention spans; I do indeed meet exceptional people—inspiring ones. One diminutive actor, a barrel of fun, but a total gentleman, strikes me as particularly likable. He takes me to the studio where he's in the process of laying tracks on a rap tune. I can't believe my ears; I go back and forth between his face and the monitors, utterly mesmerized. What takes him to go straight from a Broadway stage to this shady midtown studio to record what is essentially a black tune by right? But then again, the same could be said of the blues, or jazz—someone's got to make the leap at some point. What takes him to do it? The fun of it, period! It's sheer rebellion on the theme of positivity. You want to be a true rebel? Make your life better! That's what the guy exudes: unadulterated fun!

The actor, short of giving him a name, isn't shy on talking about his life, from the era of the silents to his present string of theater performances, via fortunes and misfortunes and many marriages. Maybe all that exuberance is his way of hiding the pain. But one wouldn't know by the way things are. I very much enjoy my time with him in spite of the ephemeralness of the encounter.

El Jay calls me from California to ask me if I'm interested in joining him in San Francisco where he'll be meeting with his agent to discuss plans for an important reunion followed by a world tour. He says it might come in handy to get acquainted with some heavy lifters in the business. San Francisco is the other city outside London which has always fascinated me. Maybe something karmic there as well...

I land at SFO on a foggy day after a pleasant flight in the company of the female passenger sitting next to me, a gorgeous red hair from the dance troupe at the ballet. She's involved but we exchange numbers all the same.

I catch a cab to the St. Francis, where I've booked a room a few doors from El Jay's. Reception informs me he's at a meeting at the Board Room on the second floor.

I meet with agents, promoters, one of the three guitarists on the bill who turns out to be a close friend of the producer who tried to sell me the house with the stream going through the living room—but no surprise there—and various figures attached to the logistics of time, places, and money. There's nothing in it for me, but I get more business cards to add to my collection.

Unlike El Jay who can't be seen in public without being accosted by some hard boiled fans, I can actually get out and enjoy the town. SF is def not like NY. For one thing, there's plenty of focus here—the present is real and touchable. The map tells me that if I walk through Chinatown, I'll reach North Beach where the sixties poets used to hang out. Always visit where the poets hole up; it's got to be a power zone!

Although the poets of importance are gone, their ghosts still hang around. You just have to follow the smell of roasted beans and swing the doors into one of the North Beach landmarks to know Gleason, Adam, or Doyle once were there.

One such place is Caffe Trieste, where I find an empty table for two. But as the place fills up, one beautiful Goddess asks me if I'm willing to share. I oblige with barely refrained enthusiasm. Honestly, I'm a bit tired of the company of men at the mo, so the refreshing presence of a member of the other sex sounds just about right.

Even though she entered with a group, she's actually by herself.

For some strange, inexplicable reason, today's date flashes through my mind as if it were imperative that it should be remembered. So, today is the 29th of January 1980, a Tuesday. El Jay informed me, nine days ago, that the Steelers had beaten the Rams in Pasadena, a sad day for L.A.! Personally, I don't give a damn about American football. What's important is today's date.

The Goddess returns with a mug of house coffee, sits down, wiggles some to loosen her jacket and scarf, and finally faces me with a corner smile.

"I'm Lisa, by the way."
"Nice to meet you, Lisa; you must be a regular."

"No, I'm new, but I was born here. You didn't tell me your name?"

I tell her my name.

"Are you French? I went to high school in Dijon."

"French from England."

"Born in England living in France, or born in France living in England?"

"The heart was born in England while the rest chose France."

"If your heart is visiting San Francisco, you could be in trouble."

"I'm here on music business—no heart—just the brain."

"Too bad, I don't do too well with brains."

"Well, that's it then!"

We laugh in chorus. I trust a form of introduction is made, but I'm not sure my sense of humor is necessary to the process. There are depths that mere repartee can't explore, so perhaps the time to both open up and listen has come.

Lisa tells me about her family, her Italian and Russian background and ancestry. She carries with her the duality of being close to her roots while simultaneously distancing herself from them. There's pain that's trying to find the surface but can't quite get there. I relate—I always relate to pain.

I tell her about my past, staying on the safe side of not saying too much too fast—"Some of the wounds are still healing," is the excuse when she probes. She doesn't seem to care much about the superficial, but I can tell she likes the fact I'm a musician, so I promise to sign a copy of the rock opera if we happen to find one at Tower

Records down Columbus Avenue, since we agree on a walk as soon as we finish with our second round of coffees.

∞∞∞∞

Indeed, we pass by Tower Records where we find the double album, but instead of taking on my offer, Lisa asks me to sign it and put it back in the rack. "I don't have a turntable," that's all she says. I dig her style.

Night and chill descend upon us. I'm not quite dressed for the weather, which is a lot colder than I had expected. Northern California isn't anything like its southern counterpart, I learn. Now I know.

Lisa lives a few blocks up the hill, on Greenwich. I walk her to her apartment. She has no phone for me to reach her, just the address. I promise I'll write. We shake hands. I start walking, stop to look back, she waves, blowing me a kiss; I blow one back. We had a great time.

It was a lie when I said only my brain traveled to San Francisco, and I'm afraid to say it's true that bringing your heart to the Golden City is asking for trouble. Just ask Mr. Bennett.

My walk back to the hotel is accompanied by a mixed bag of emotions for the woman I just met and the city that seems to want more of me. I know I will return, but the reality of work and logistics calls me back to the fold. El jay and I are flying back to London tomorrow, and I'd better start taking care of my affairs as soon as I get home. Money doesn't grow on trees, as the saying goes, and time is of the essence when one knows the door of opportunity doesn't stay open for long. I need a gig with a touring band, or at least, some studio work.

First comes the studio work. It turns out, in some predictable way, that the band's guitarist can't quite cut his part, so I get the call. They're a bunch of young lads, who just got signed on a major because their style's in. But the producer, without quite reminding them that the advent of punk is behind us, insists on a modicum of talent. There's no competition; I do my thing and I'm out of there. No credits, just cash—it suits me fine.

Actually, it suits me so fine that I get more calls, and then some more. Not only can I pay for the remaining on the house, but I've got my eyes on a near-mint Helios mixing board as well.

Before long, the Helios is joined by a 24 track Studer. Easy does it, because the stuff's quite dear. I'm in no rush to get buried in debts.

As sessions lead to others, I'm called across the channel to record at the Chateau, which isn't as hot as its legendary past. Time has a way of wilting things after it gives them a chance to bloom—everything's a cycle.

In the meantime, my song catalogue is growing and I'm antsy to gig. I've got the rehearsal space in Camden, plus the studio's almost there. It's just a matter of acquiring a few high-end mikes, but I'm not quite there yet financially. I also put a few quid down on some council houses which I'm having work done on. As I said, I'm hopeful the market will make a three-sixty, especially since continental money is moving in. The problem with the Camden house is that it's big and I'm single. I'm not really interested in the women that cross my way; once again, the drugs and the heavy drinking are the issue. I can't function if my head isn't clear, and much less love from an authentic place. In other words, I hate fucking for the sake of fucking. To be perfectly honest, I can't get it up. Call me a hopeless romantic!

I think about Lisa in San Francisco—it's time to write.

I finally put a band together and cut a few demos of my songs that my agent's shopping around. I'm glad I invested in the studio; it makes things so much easier. The engineer's a friend I met through El Jay a couple of years ago and he lives up in Hampstead which isn't far. I think the demos are great; the band totally coalesces on them, and I would be surprised if some label didn't show interest. But you never know in this day and age. I've got the publishing all sorted out—I'm giving nothing away. Sorry bean counters!

Lisa wrote back; I haven't had time to open her letter yet. I want to make sure I'm comfy before I get to read her. I'm not normally excited about personal mail, but I am in her case.

The letter is short, mostly thanking me for the company. I sense she's not expecting to see me for some time, if ever, which might explain the lack of emotional commitment to her words. She got a job at a bookstore, but I don't perceive she's too thrilled about it. It's not a sad letter, but it's not a happy one either; rather, it carries its message through what is not being said. I don't want it to be projection on my part, but I can't help getting the impression that she's trying to say something that doesn't make it to the surface. It's interesting because it's an item that showed up at our meeting regarding pain. It's more like she's trying to be aware of it, but it's hiding from her. I know it's a lot of underlying for a short letter, so I could easily be overshooting it, but then again... Maybe it's the lack of resolve about it. Did I expect something more? That makes me want to investigate. But then the phone rings.

"Hi there, I just got a phone. Did you get my mail?"

That stops me short in my thinking.

"Hey, Lisa, yeah, I just finished reading it. How's life?"

"Well, aside from the job, nothing too exciting since we met. I've made a few friends, but no strings attached."

"How's your grandma?"

"She's doing well, thanks for asking! I'm so happy to have her in my life—one of the major reasons why I'm here."

"Any prospects on the love front, or is that too personal?"

"It all depends on why you're asking."

"I figure a Goddess shouldn't be loveless for too long, that's why."

"What makes you think I'm loveless?"

"Because it's the first thing people in love call about, otherwise they don't call at all."

"You have an odd way of looking at people, mister, but no, nothing as good as romance. Now, since you ask?"

"Well, I wrote, didn't I?"

"I think you can do better."

"Better than write?"

"No, better than evading my question."

"I felt loveless until you called; what about that?"

"OK, much better, whoa!"

"And?"

"I like you too, if that's where we're at."

"We both walked into it, I guess; but thanks—I like the sound of it."

"I knew I was in trouble when we met. Luckily, we live too far apart for it to happen."

"I take it that you don't believe in long distance relationships."

"Long distance friendships make sense, but relationships, like what, phone sex?"

"I wouldn't be so rude as to suggest it; I was just asking for the sake of contemplating the options. I guess it calls for another visit."

"You're not thinking of coming back to San Francisco, are you?"

"Or you could be visiting London...?"

"I just started a new job and I'm finally settling in my place, plus I'm not financially capable; so, I don't see how I would be willing to do that."

"A straight answer deserving of my respect—one new reason to like you even more."

"I'm not sure what you mean by that... It's not that I don't want to visit London—I've never been to England—but the timing isn't so great."

"I get it. Maybe I can mix business with pleasure—I'll check with my agent and let you know if San Francisco is on the list of possibilities."

We hang up. The room feels suddenly warmer. I think I'm in love.

10 – NEW YORK & SAN FRANCISCO

The labels like the demo, but fail to commit out of reasons as disparate as the entire spectrum of bullshit.

"Not New Wave enough!" "Too seventies!" "You should market it in America!" "Guitar-oriented music is on its way out!" "Your need to add synthesizers!" The list goes on... Sure, my music's nothing like what my good friends—with their reggae or ska leanings—are putting out, but it's plenty novel in many ways. It's hard to let go of a documented history of reluctance to embrace what's not considered marketable, even though the same history has proven over and over again that said reluctance is a sure way to cut one's throat. It's the fear factor again, that of committing to a vision rather than profitability. Everybody loves and needs money, but not everybody understands that it doesn't buy integrity—the more the desire to gain, the farther the shift of the moral compass.

Now, of course, I could be overrating my work, but the band's live traction is indisputable, even the A&R reps that come to see us say so.

I got it from a number of artistes that the majors don't like to sign business-minded songwriters. In other words, they'd rather own the publishing rights, or at least half of them; thus turning intellectual property into a form of exclusive licensing. It's incredible the gall of these people in the face of outright robbery. Now, thinking of it, the western world is built on robbery. In the end, it's a matter of whether one treats life as business as usual or not. I personally don't, but I can see where that could work against you, like for me right now.

I can't say that I'm not disappointed in the response, but then again, I fancy seeing life as my own creation, which means that I either change my approach to doing business or reconfigure my beliefs in regard to the rights and wrongs of going at it; which sounds like the same but isn't. I'm never gonna be able to honestly say that there never was robbery in the world, but I could outwit the bandits by tweaking the old overlook. In other words, I don't have to make the faults of the system an emotional reality at my end—I shall be like mothers loving their children in spite of their handicaps. I'm talking about the art of compassion for the wicked here. It sounds mischievous, but I'm serious.

Whether my change of outlook has anything to do with it or not, one of the majors suggests that my agent submits the demos to their New York A&R department.

I get the call that one of their reps is on her way to join the band for the short stretch of our continental tour opening for a famous Aussie act. Can management accommodate her? The business mind is management, or me; and yes, I shall be glad to accommodate her—my house's big enough and so is the shared tour bus.

The she in question is a young, wiry thing that talks at me rather than to me. I guess she's on a mission. She has ideas that don't necessarily line up with mine, but I'll let the music and the crowd do the talking and we'll see what comes out of it. She really would like to run the show—but she can't—so she broods until the mates come in. Unlike the guys in the last band, who, one might say, were chauvinist pigs, this bunch is composed of genuinely good men without an ounce of prejudice in their bones—I made sure of that during audition—and it relaxes the atmosphere around the agent. Now, I realize that she actually was apprehensive in the light of the potential of being diminished by yet the obligatory demonstration of mostly reflexive brawn so prevalent in rock music.

It turns out that—Jenny's her name—is a fun, intelligent female that makes for good company. I'm sure we'll get along very well while touring. It's actually a mini European tour, until the next opener latches on for the Asian leg of the main act's world journey—so, no heavy strain on the relationship.

I was far from expecting that our Jenny and the bassist would find a liking for each other; and what a liking, friends! Now the guy wants to move to New York, something that sticks out as a fundamental compromise to the plan of getting signed by the label; unless, of course, the whole band moves there as well, which, naturally, the other two members oppose. My brain hurts!

But life being full of surprises, one knows how to go with the flow. We get signed anyway, and a new bassist is brought in.

I don't know what to say to Lisa. There's no way I can make it to San Francisco while in the process of negotiating contracts, scheduling interviews, and recording and producing an album on top of it. Perhaps it's time to get some help!

Help comes in the form of Jenny asking the band to record the album at Unique in Manhattan. I'm also relieved of production duty since an ace producer has made himself available after having heard the demo. I'm somewhat miffed by it, but I see her point. It's just that it's going to cost a lot more out of the royalties, but I'm told that royalties have a better chance to exist in the first place with a killer sound and a house name behind it. I can't argue with the obvious. Oddly, the new bassist bails out and the previous one returns to the fold. I'm sure Jenny has something to do with it. It's the way the cookie crumbles in rock and roll. It also demonstrates that I can't control everything.

I inform Lisa about the schedule. She takes it philosophically like someone who always knew of the difficulties involved in long distance visiting. I'm not saying that she sounds resigned to the obvious doom looming over our embryonic relationship, but there's something of the, "Well, we had a good few hours together, so she should feel blessed," that rings of terminality. Even from New York, San Francisco feels so far away, that it might as well belong to another world. Actually, now that I think of it, it does. Its people are so different, so much more easy-going and welcoming than those of any city I've lived in, that I fancy imagining them as visitors from other planets. They probably are.

I tell Lisa about my theory, but her mind is somewhere else, like she's thinking, "So what's going to happen now?"

I know of the many that left their labors of love to build families, taking the odd jobs as accountants, supermarket clerks, lorry drivers; some of the luckier ones as supervisors, or even the rare music executive. I still have to meet one who hasn't regretted the move, and years later, tried to have a go at music again. Mind you, since I'm in the business, I only meet those with regrets— perhaps there are not as many as I think... My point is that I will never compromise my career for a relationship. I was born with music in my head, remember?

Now, of course, we all need someone in our lives, and there's always the potential of making dire choices that may lead to catastrophic consequences. I like Lisa, which in my heart is as good as love, since I have liked very few women, except perhaps for my ex-drummer's girlfriend, way back when, and my first love with her way-pre-punk, punk looks. In other words, the scale is holding a precarious balance between the emotional qualitative and the common rationale. It's a lot like choosing between music and a straight job, but a notch above.

But reason sees it otherwise. Why not ask Lisa how she fits in a relationship with a musician on a busy schedule? So, I ask.

"As long as I can see my nonna on a regular basis, I don't mind the bohemian lifestyle, I'm an artiste too, remember? Although, for now, I'm still sorting my life out, and it's probably not a good idea to not finish what I've started. And just in case you forgot, we really don't know each other. So, before I say yes or no, I need to think about it. I'm also contemplating signing up for a couple of classes at San Francisco State. But I like you, mister, so let's not rush this, OK?"

I like the first and last parts better than the middle one, especially the end. "Let's not rush this" rings of hope and looks of sunshine. Reason always wins in the end, even if it takes its sweet time to arrive. In the midst of the conversation, I promise to hop on a plane to San Francisco during a couple of days off from recording. I can crash at her place, Lisa offers.

The recording goes extremely well. I miss my trusted Hiwatt but I'm impressed with the resident Roland JC 120—for once, a solid state guitar amp that doesn't suck! But the gear is inconsequential; what matters is the energy that comes across. I think the guys put all they had in the material and it shows. Everybody's happy with the results and we're off to the next phase of preparing for what reviews and airplay have to say.

Well, I lied. I couldn't free any time until the production stage, and only because the producer required some space before he could let the band back in for their feedback. But Lisa's fine with it—she understands. Life is life regardless of how you shake it—it always comes with its last minute change-orders.

She can't make it to the airport because of her work, but she will be home by the time I get there. I know my way around.

Just as the cab drops me at the foot of her apartment building, she comes running, or more like dance-running. She's full of life and happiness—

definitely one of the aliens! This time it's hugs instead of handshakes. Could it be our relationship improved without any of the physical proximity? I guess so, and it's magical!

I drop my things, and since we're both hungry, we immediately go out to check our dining options. It's a toss between Italian and Chinese. First we go for Chinese but then change our minds as we get transmogrified by the smell of garlic emanating from an Italian kitchen. Italian it is!

The *how are yous* are followed by the *nice to see yous* and the *what are you up tos*; all generously served with smiles and misty eyes. If it sounds like I'm making fun of the process of getting reacquainted with each other—well, I'm not—it's only because what's next is more important. What's next defines depth; whether we have more to say or not; whether we are going to take chances or cower under the mundane; or, whether we can comfortably look each other in the eyes—and stay there—or shift glances in fear of revealing what we seek to hide.

What's next is as scrumptious as the meal—we are two open books, as open as the fragrance of wild-crafted herbs. You just can't put an Italian woman and a Frenchman at a dinner table without the predictable culinary cross-reference, regardless of whether the Italian is a U.S. denizen or the French an Anglophobe. We silently approve of the corniness of it. Maybe it's the Chianti, or the whole of Italy, but we end up holding hands before the tiramisus are served. Like a promise, or an unwritten contract of trust and faith in the unknown, the future is telling us to hold tight, that things are on their best behavior. I believe the message and I trust Lisa does too. After paying and thanking the waiter, we're on a walk to the bay. Unlike the first time, the evening is a balmy, fogless affairs still bathed in daylight. The sun sets below the Golden Gate Bridge, now a perpendicular gate into a different kind of unknown, a place you walk in after a job well done, perhaps. We're holding hands like young brothers and sisters, or a couple in their golden years. We exist between times, in a perfect moment. Just then, Lisa leans against me as if to say, "I feel safe with you." It doesn't take long before we kiss, as the sun leaves its purple veil above the horizon.

We could go straight to her place and make love, but the night is young and it's Friday. I propose we go see the DKs at the *Fab Mab*, but it turns out neither of us is really into getting trampled by the extreme exuberance of unleashed anger, even if justified. Seeing the line outside settles the deal. I guess we're off to the cinemas since it's second on the list. I can tell Lisa loves flicks by the excitement in her voice when I propose we check out the Blues Brothers, which has just been released.

Turns out the film is fun and full of great music—the perfect accompaniment to a fine meal and an even finer walk; especially when topped by a few make-out breaks along the way to the apartment. One may say that I'm doing an excellent job at leaving my heart in San Francisco.

What follows may be best described as the most complete sexual experience I've ever had. Sorry girls, but this Goddess knows her stuff! She likes it au naturel, free of gimmickry and pretence—it's sex for sex's sake in a bath of pure loving. Please, excuse the descriptive, but I don't recollect ever getting so aroused in my life. Lisa's gorgeous, delicious, passionate, and above all, so fucking genuine that I wonder how sex can exist without that kind of authenticity. So, now I know why the groupies never did it for me—no bad feelings, Mesdames, I love you all the same!

We get up at noon right after reaching Nirvana for like the sixth time. My return flight's at four, so plenty of time to shower and have breakfast at a corner bistro.

Of course, it's much too short, but I can't stress enough how vital this visit is to our relationship. When Lisa says, "I'm so glad you came—I had lost track of whether we were for real or not," I understand exactly what she means. We are surrounded by probabilities eager to turn hopes into missed opportunities. All it takes is one distraction, one instance of carelessness, to make one long for what is gone.

Airplay kicks in strongly in both the U.S. and Europe for two of the tunes with the most commercial appeal; in other words, the ones I specifically wrote for that purpose, so that we could play out of the box for the rest of the album. Of course, the label wants more of them; thus I loosely promise more for the next three albums of the contract. Jenny's OK with that. The most important news to arrive is Swen's Rolling Stone review that lifts the album at one of the bests of the year. My respect goes to the man for his kindness—I'm humbled.

Before we hit the road for the European tour, I visit San Francisco one more time. Passions are unleashed

with unbound vitality. I don't see how we're not going to
want to be with each other in spite of the obstacles. Lisa's
even open to checking London one of these days. It's
again a short stay, but a great one. Now, I want to marry
the woman!

11 – MAKE OR BREAK

In spite of all the promo and the promises, the album doesn't fare quite as expected. It's more of an issue with Jenny than it is for us—we're OK with the respectable amount of sales and the money that has been trickling in, especially at the songwriter's end. The label doesn't want to take a risk with a U.S. tour, even as an opener, but that's not for them to say. The lack of exposure doesn't sell albums, they know it darn well. It's just that management is going through a reshuffle and Jenny's job is on the line—that kind of complication.

In the end it's all math, with the bean counters on one side trying to steal the beans, and the band on the other trying to hold onto them.

It turns out that my friendship with El Jay and my collection of business cards has some leverage in the matter. Even though the label claims we're delinquent on the advance, I deem that abandoning the band at this point is cause for the losses. We need to play the United States, that's all; plus I have my reasons to want to be in America, especially the West Coast.

We're all fine with opening for a major act, and thus, it is arranged that for twelve of the States' most major venues, we're filling in for a group with a temporarily ailing singer. And on we go, with barely enough time to pack before lifting off the tarmac. I didn't even bring a spare guitar, just the Paul I bought in the old country. Same with the rest of the gear—I cross my fingers. It's worse for the drummer who's gonna have to play someone else's tubs. Thinking of it, it's a make or break situation. At least, it's based on determination rather than desperation. Overall, we're excited!

The final three cities of the tour are, in order, Los Angeles, San Francisco, and Seattle, with a three-day break between the last two. It means another chance to spend time with my love, and I couldn't be more pleased with the arrangement.

The tour, speaking of it, has been simply awesome. With audiences screaming for encores, we got the attention of the media, consequently boosting the sales of the record. Out of the blue, we're in the Billboard top 50 albums, with a top ten single and another on its tail. I think it awakens the label into liking us and Jenny can now keep her job. I always thought the human race had the patent on irony—I'm proven correct once again.

As I work the abacus down in L.A., I observe that between the various music-based incomes and the rent revenues on the two Camden houses and the recording studio, I'm building the kind of capital that I think needs investing in something other than British. I've always sensed the real estate business was leaning towards a wild swing in favor of property owners, and the feeling is all the more acute now that Hong Kong fortunes are on the brink of flooding the entire North American west coast. How do I know that? I pay attention and hear the messenger winds. It doesn't hurt to glance at the business section of the dailies once in a while either. So, the idea of buying a house in San Francisco doesn't appear so unrealistic at this point. I'll bring it to Lisa's attention and see what she thinks, but the more I look at it, the more triumphant it gets.

The San Francisco break comes as the result of the Sacramento venue having been cancelled due to an administrative error that ended up booking two acts on the same date. I can't attest to that kind of mishap being endemic to the business, but knowing rock and roll, it comes across more as a matter of going with the punches and forging ahead, than something one should make a big deal about. And just about like every other mistake, it comes with its silver lining, which in this case allows me to spend time with a loved one, and for the main band to take an extended rest before hitting Japan. I could think of a worse place to get stuck in for three days.

Lisa gets to meet the bandmates as well as a couple of the guys in the main act. Her charms make her an instant, radiating center of harmony wherever she goes. She doesn't give a fuck about the status of legends, or whatever comes with the wickedness of adulation—she makes the dudes feel at ease, giving them a reason to be normal people with normal needs, such as those of not feeling like freaks when they go out.

She loves the idea of me buying a house in the area, but doesn't quite get that the way I see it, we're buying a house together. When she finally grasps where I'm at, she seems touched, but she doesn't put on the act of knee-jerking in one direction or the other; instead, she waits for me to say something. And since I too wait for her to speak, an odd silence is formed that is cause for the both of us bursting in laughter.

My idea of a house is something with a bunch of rooms, a couple of baths, an attic, a basement, a garage if possible, and some sort of view, preferably one not looking directly into the neighbor's bathroom.

Lisa's choice is one of a colorful cottage on Telegraph Hill—small and cozy—with a great view of the Bay looking towards the Golden Gate. It's also desirable that it comes with a small garden.

Her vision is akin to a painting I see for the first time, in which I discover a landscape forgotten long ago. It changes my whole approach to perceiving my surroundings. It no longer is about a statement of convenience in broad, gaudy strokes, but rather, about quality, in precise, pointillistic minuteness. It also explains why she's a painter.

I decide to return to San Francisco after the Seattle show. I call Neil, the engineer, asking him to keep an eye on my Camden property for another week. He doesn't mind—he practically lives there, working in the studio, wiring the equipment we purchased before I left. I can't wait to check the plate reverb he's installing in the new, dedicated basement room. I also call Jenny in New York to let her know where to reach me in case the label wants to talk to me. But to be honest, I'd like to get a break from it all and rest my bones in the cradle of loving arms and legs.

The Seattle gig was our best, and so it was for the main act, who wishes we could have stayed for the Asian and South American legs of their world tour. There will always be other times to cross paths; after all, the UK is a small place. As we exchange phone numbers and addresses, I'm surprised by how many of them have homes in the States. I guess musical minds think alike.

I'm barely back at Lisa's place when Jenny calls to inform me that the album went gold. I fucking knew it!

While I was in Seattle, Lisa spotted a quaint little house in need of TLC on Telegraph hill. Being used to fixing wrecks in London, I prepare for the worse.

It turns out that Lisa's view of something in need of love means that it could improve with her personal touch; aside from that the house is perfectly fine as it is. Actually, it's a beauty tucked amid ample, carefully-kept-wild vegetation. One may call it a candy box, but it's probably an unfair evaluation coming from an eye used to, mostly, the gray monochromes of industrial Northern Europe. Actually I'm wrong; we've got colorful canal houseboats by the Stables Market in Camden.

The real estate agent takes us around the place. We're not the only ones, so I assume there's gonna be some bidding involved. Now, that I'm past the shock of the sticker price, I'm comfortable with the idea. I'm no speculator—I'm not in it to make money—but I favor a healthy market over a dead one. Judging by how popular the area is, I know a sound investment when I see one. A quick ballpark calculation brings me within a fifth of its future value, just from the fact that the Hong Kong handover is merely fifteen years ahead. I guess living in the UK has sensitized me to it. I mean, really; it doesn't take a genius to realize where this is about to go. There's no way the cash is going the mainland China—and I'm talking cash by the boatload—so, where will it go? Into real estate, baby—real estate, in Canada and the U.S.!

OK, I'm losing it, while Lisa's checking the rooms and the views. I reckon I have a calling as a financier, but it's not all lost since I do my own books, effectively keeping the sharks at bay.

I'm not totally obsessed with figures; I love the place too. I imagine the two of us with a bunch of kids; it could be tight but manageable, but I'm ahead of myself...

"So, what do you think, love?" I ask.
"What about you?"
"I'm asking first."
"I'm not going to love it if you don't."
"Me neither."

We both love it, obviously!

There are indeed a couple of bids involved, but there's no way I'm going to let it go, especially when I already see the two of us living in it. Plus, I don't see the logic in blowing its market value at the mo—it's not a buyers market, not quite yet. The competition consists of people like us, not banks. It's all contingent on who loves the place most; it's the calculus of emotions, of idyllic visions, of poetry and romanticism, and no-one's gonna beat us at it. Mind you, it doesn't hurt to be able to pay in full; it makes it easier at the level of the paperwork. No mortgage, no banks, just two names on the title and a discreet shared account at one of the local credit unions—well, in a nutshell, that is. I'm sparing you the details.

I'm sort of all over the map. After seeing the Telegraph Hill house, I had to return to London to take care of my affairs on the home front; home being the big house with the recording studio, of course, but where is home these days? And just there, it truly gets complicated. It's the grand clash of heart and mind, the dichotomy of the material and spiritual. I need my shit around me, meaning my gear, my rehearsal space, my 24 track studio with the glorious EMT plate reverb in the basement. What am I going to do, abandon my stuff so that my heart can find a cocoon to soothe all the aches of the past? Now comes the time to assess the playing field without freaking out!

For one, there's no way I'm letting go of the London house. The other twos are rentals—I don't care about those; my management company is already taking care of rent and repairs. I call Neil up in Hempstead. I know he's renting; perhaps I can interest him in some kind of business arrangement with the recording studio. For security reasons, someone needs to be there at all times—London's full of thieves and everyone knows music gear is the highest commodity on the black market.

We set up a meeting at our favorite Young's pub. Neil's into it. We settle on a loose contract until we hone the details. He rents the bottom half of the house, leaving the upstairs for me and Lisa—it's like two separate living units anyway—while he books and maintain the studio on a 60/40 split of the net, me getting the forty.

Perhaps there's no need to explain, but the house is so large that even with the studio taking half the space, the bottom floor leaves plenty of room for a comfortable two bedroom apartment, which Neil and his wife, Fuzzy, find to their liking. Since I spent a bundle on soundproofing, no-one's going to suffer from the noise. We also decide to install a security system, making me realize that I should have done it a long time ago.

In the meantime the record is still climbing.

I'm back in San Francisco, keys in hand to open our love pad for the first time. It's the 21st of September 1980 and so much has happened since that pivotal date in January when Lisa and I accidentally bumped into each other. But was it really an accident? I would put my chips on a long-planned affair, orchestrated from an inconceivable place if there were such a betting table. In fact, I don't believe in accidents—there's purpose in everything—it's all about paying attention and getting the timing right. I fancy creating my own reality—it's empowering and fun. It's like jumping off a tall cliff, shouting *hee haw!*, trusting you're going to grow wings before hitting the ground. In reality, the ground never comes, wings or not, and you're like a child absorbing the never-ending joys of life's playground. Some say I'm a ridiculous optimist, that life is full of ambushes, like sickness, misfortunes, or just bad luck. What is luck anyway? And who said a playground was safe? It's all rhetorics—yours against mine, mine against theirs—blah, blah, blah! Oh my, ha ha! OK, as I was saying, we're moving into the Telegraph Hill house. I brought my Les

Paul Deluxe, the Princeton, a couple of pedals, and my Revox reel to reel over from London. They will stay here, but it's as much as the space allows. It's nice to have a few familiar things around, as to bridge the old and new. I'm also known to freak out when a guitar isn't in the line of sight.

∞∞∞

It takes some conviction to get Lisa comfortable with the idea of installing an alarm system in the new house. I understand her point about paranoia, but there still are reasons why one shouldn't leave a house all by itself when gone for more than a day. The fact is we're flying to London in five days for a two-week—can I say vacation?—and it's nice not to have to wonder whether or not your stuff will be there upon return. She gets it—it's just healthy repartees between us, anyway.

Whether Lisa likes London or not is a matter of perspective. Take her to Regent's park and she's in heaven, Trafalgar Square, not so much. She likes Camden Town and the big house though. It's understandable that when visiting such a huge city for the first time, one may want to stay close to the familiar for a while before exploring in safe increments, but everything changes when I take Lisa to the Tate—she finds home. Before long she's by herself in Covent Garden, checking apothecary rose salves and biological goodies at Neal's Yard, walking the old market for jewelries, inventorying theaters and plays, or going through miles of bookshelves at Foyles. In other words, the familiar grows in scope, to which the peripheral unknown sticks until it becomes absorbed. Bit by bit, the London spirit expands from the house outwards. Soon, it reaches the Thames and the bridges that cross into Lambeth, Battersea, Wandsworth; and then it's west to Kensington and Chelsea. Before long, Lisa suggests Wimbledon and Kingston, and in no time, we're driving along the coast between Portsmouth and Brighton. The London visit turns into a tour of Southern Britain.

While the bassist's in town since we're about to embark on a UK tour, we begin recording the next batch of songs at the house, with Neil at the mixing board. That was the point of building the studio in the first place—independence. If need be, we can always go somewhere else for the final mix, but as it turns out, the producer of the first album is willing to fly over, providing we book him now. Date is set for March 1st.

Lisa had a great time. She's not leaving for San Francisco without having put her personal touch to the upstairs apartment, courtesy of the artists at the Stables. As soon as the tour's over, we'll be back together on Telegraph Hill. Coincidentally, I'm invited to join a local act for the recording of his next album at the Record Plant in Sausalito. I love impeccable timing, as it's been the case since I moved to the UK in 76'—why I've always thought I should have been born here. Instead, I was *re-born* here, which is the next best thing. Mind you, I might have to look a bit deeper into that assessment, because with Lisa around, a lot of what I thought was true has turned out to be a bunch of unchecked assumptions. Beware the silent belief that shapes one's life in spite of the self's best intentions at gaining clarity. Self-hypnosis—as I trust it is—is a powerful tool that is used ever so deliberately. It's the longest con in existence, with an indefinite shelf life, as in the most toxic of substances.

Overall, I can say it's been a great run. I didn't self-destruct as I thought I was going to after the army. I didn't end up on the street, or locked in a terminal marriage like my parents, with kids I despised for having stolen the joy out of life. I didn't run away from my core issues—rather, I embraced them as my own to resolve and grow out of. It gives me a sense of pride to look at these basic accomplishments, basic in the way that anyone can make the choice to not blame the world for what they own—what they create for themselves— whether consciously or not. As I've already said, we're not here by accident—or I'll keep it personal—I'm not here by accident, regardless of my past and the many times I have said I landed in the wrong place. No, it was a choice; I landed in the right place even if it looked like the wrong one. All the fucked up past was what I had to work with to get where I am right now. No mistake, no blame, now is the time to look at the old folks from a new standpoint and forgive—it's the only way—the right way.

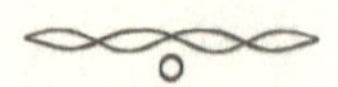

12 – DILEMMA OF TWO CITIES

I'm tracking the lead guitar on the last song of the second album when the call comes in announcing that Dave, the drummer, has died in a car accident. It's a total shock, the guy was a prince. His wife, Chrissie, is devastated, and so are Andy, the rhythm guitarist, Herbie, the bassist, and Jenny, whom I ring in New York with the news. It's bad. Neil and I look at each other in disbelief. Less than two hours ago, we were listening to the drum tracks, commenting on Dave's ace playing. What a fucking bummer! Just as we finished the UK tour too! He leaves us, accomplished, dignified in his walk into the sunset. Of course, I'm sure Chrissie is missing on the nuance, the poor thing... There is no beginning and end for her, just an elongated void until the time comes to be reunited with her man in that place that cradles eternal hearts. I have no doubt Dave will receive her with flowers—the wild ones that grow along the road to forever.

Lisa is flying over to spend time with Chrissie—an auspicious arrangement in a not so auspicious time, but there's no better healer than Lisa and her boundless love for humanity, especially in situations that call for extreme kindness.

Dave's passing poses all sorts of logistical problems that will need to be addressed when the dust settles. For now, the last thing on my mind is to look towards the future. The present is the big attention seeker, with rock papers calling for interviews and last words, and promoters whining about getting compensated for gig cancellations—the usual mayhem that comes in the aftermath of departures, and which, for some reason, always involves money. I can't imagine what Chrissie will have to deal with down the line. The job for Andy, Herbie, and me is to make sure she doesn't get screwed out of the royalty checks.

If it weren't for the record contract, I would call it quit and move to San Francisco permanently. It's the kind of emotional state I'm in right now. No, I'm not sad about Dave—we all die—but it is in the sense of fatigue that comes in the wake of realizing that accomplishment isn't measured in the one thing we do well, but rather in the compound achievements of all things human that I find my discomfort. What is my contribution to the world in which we live? Is it in the form of fame and enlightenment of the masses via ridiculously simple lyrics over riffing and clever arrangements, or is it something far more subtle that touches fewer hearts, but with much more lasting and rippling effects? But do I even need to think about these things, as if I were at the center of everyone's private universe? How presumptuous and vanitous to think I can make a difference in lives, before even considering whether or not I am capable of addressing my own issues and generating enough love to fill our little house on Telegraph Hill! The mind can be your best friend and your worst ally in one swell thought.

But I find comfort in having Lisa around. I guess I'd better admit that I feel fragile right now; a lot like the child that never was truly loved, but who puts on this cover of toughness, as it to say he doesn't need the kindness he silently craves. Melancholia is a tide that comes with the dead body of the unfulfilled, the regrets attached to the lost, and the recognition that with the passing of time, things are further and further removed from the realm of possibilities. Dave's death brings me to the brink of my own potential unraveling, forcing me to look into the depths of my past torments and see how much the whole lot is still there, merely put aside in all of its restlessness. It brings me in line with the fact that swapping countries and lifestyles is nothing more than running away from the things I fear. The only one thing that, on the other hand, isn't part of the escape, is my relationship with Lisa. It is the true redemption, the metamorphosis of the love negated into the one given—my chance at making good with the mess.

I'm far from saying that England, the house in Camden, the band, Neil and the studio, the record deal, etcetera are all for naught—that would be sheer insanity—but it's true that I have been distracted by the material at the cost of managing my emotional reality. And so, now couldn't be a better time to break down the institution of denial and open the space for something a lot more outwardly.

Herbie, Andy, and I aren't into replacing Dave—Dave's irreplaceable. I'm not just talking about his drumming—there are plenty of good players out there that can fill his shoes—but about his heart. One simply doesn't replace Dave's heart! So, we decide to go with a studio cat for the next albums and hire a temp for the gigs. Maybe, over time, someone will fit in naturally.

But it's not just Dave's passing that complicates things, there's also the fact that Andy's in Dublin, Herbie in New York, and I'm bouncing between London and San Francisco. I tried to coerce Jenny into moving west but her ties to the label prevent her from doing so. Herb, Andy, and I are now like one of the many bands separated by land and sea, joining whenever corporate reality rings to remind us we're under contract. But I'm ahead of myself—we're not there and likely will never be.

What it's coming down to at this point between Lisa and I is, "Where do we choose to make our home?" I first thought that we could have two, but it seems more and more unrealistic as time goes, particularly since Lisa wants to stay close to her grandmother in San Fran. I'm concerned about not being able to sustain a healthy relationship while my job keeps us apart. I love my partner too much to jeopardize our precious connection, yet the thing is that, whichever way I shake it, I have to commute between continents if I plan on remaining in the business, and of course, touring is inevitable.

The situation stirs emotions in discomforting waves. It's a dilemma that has affected many of my peers and which, in spite of many attempts at resolve, has destroyed careers or marriages—and sometimes both.

Thankfully, Lisa isn't needy enough to demand I relinquish my lifestyle so that she can have me by her side, to the contrary. But I know too well, through the channels of intuition, that no-one is fully immune to the effect of distance and solitude. For someone like me who enjoys a busy schedule, it's easy to ignore the emotional loneliness and the time that elapses in long stretches. It only hits me at the snap of reconnecting with the present, when the mind find itself naked in a surprise moment of clarity after having returned to the body from a journey of pseudo-importance—a stepping off the stage of sort at the end of the act—but soon ready to resume with the next leg of that never-ending road—or play.

Lisa is off the stage, watching as I appear from the wings, only to disappear again, visible but untouchable—a familiar face amidst an elusive curtain play of little significance, all artificial—all so removed from any form of emotional center of gravity.

Art may imitate life, but at no time should it become a substitute for it. It's where I'm at right now, awake and confused.

Where do I fit in the context of being in love with two cities thousands of miles apart? It's a hard question bereft of logical answers. If I were to rationalize, I would say that London saved my life, while San Francisco promises a better one. Why can't they just be—like in dreams—one and the same? Oh, sweet and sour dilemma!

Lisa's my life partner, but only as long as I'm available. It doesn't take a genius to understand that someone like her—a free spirit—isn't tethered to the feeble post of fickleness. As much as she loves our house on the hill, I can easily see her move out, briefly turn around to look at me from the distance, blow a kiss, and then be gone to never be seen again. It's a painful projection that I hope will never materialize.

I don't let a day pass without calling. Lisa loves the house, but she can't hide the sentiment that she prefers it with me in it.

"I imagine you playing your guitar by the window, looking at the city from our nest," she says.

How can I not melt to that? I so too would like to be in that picture! But there's a cost to bear with it in the realization that it can only exist in a butterfly moment. We're all well aware that what I do is what allows for the picture to exist in the first place.

"I'm there is spirit, love!"

What else can I say?

Even though I believe from the depth of my heart that no problem ever comes without its solution encrypted within it, I pray for a resolve to our issue. It's part of the exercise, which brings me to look into what I might be holding to, to allow for such dilemma.

The one thing that pins me to London is the studio. It's my brainchild on top of being a sizable investment. I could ship the gear to the States at a prohibitive cost, but it can be done. On the other hand, I could sell the big house and the studio as a package and get my money's worth. Considering that similar gear is readily available in the Bay Area and Los Angeles, it may be wise to go that route and build a new studio in San Francisco. The idea grips like Velcro. I guess it just suffices to think hard enough about it. Now, I must present it to Neil and see what kind of reaction it generates.

As it turns out, Neil had also been thinking about it. My proposal of him buying me out as a business partner meets his projection of turning the house into a commercial facility. In other words, he's super interested in purchasing the whole thing providing the price is right.

The right price is when I come up on top of my investment by the slightest layer of cream. Neil and I only have a loose agreement, hence no contract. The only binding arrangement is the lease on the downstairs apartment. I've never kept tabs on how much money the rental of the studio added up to, trusting Neil with it, plus I silently wanted him to collect as much as he could, since he did all the work and also because he's one of my best friends. The idea of the studio has always been for me and the band to have the freedom to practice and record any time we wished, but now, with Dave gone, things are different, and realistically, they've come to an end.

With the help of a few investors in the business, Neil becomes the rightful owner of *Calibration Studios*. And thus goes the Camden house and the delightful upstairs apartment, where Lisa and I spent many a night enjoying each other's company among the naughty things we did with every suitable excuse. I don't have to mention the wild sex, but that's the part I never want to forget about, so be it!

Without my pied-à-terre in London, I'm now free to make San Francisco my home; meaning I must propose in order to apply for a green card.

Lisa beats me to it by saying, "I've got no choice but to marry you!"

When it comes to the heart, there's no contest—might as well get used to it!

We wed at City Hall on a glorious November day of 1981, more precisely, Thursday the 12th. I wanted the ceremony to be tomorrow, Friday, but the winds of superstition worked against me. Lisa's nonna is all smiles. El Jay, Herbie and Jenny, Andy, Neil and Fuzzy, Chrissie and her new boyfriend, and half the poets of North Beach join us for the reception, where a stage has been built for the obligatory jam. Dave is no doubt among us laughing his big bear laugh. No time has ever been this exquisite.

13 – THE CUBE

It takes me a while to get the gears to mesh in the Bay Area, but as soon as they do, it's hard to stop the momentum.

The one thing that jumps at me is the number of UK nationals I meet in town. I was well aware of the L.A. and Sarasota communities of British rockers, but it kind of surprises me to discover another in the Bay Area. I make the acquaintance of Dave K, a well respected keyboard player, who connects me with Ric, a fabulous drummer, with whom I had briefly crossed paths at the Marquee in London, while sharing the stage. Ric is on for joining the band for the recording of the third album, and potentially doing the promotional tour.

I was meant to mention that the second record is going strong and recently went gold. We just finished playing the U.S. and are due for a month in Europe. Somehow, we haven't quite broken into the Asian and South American market, but without shooting myself in the foot, I'm somewhat relieved by it. I'm not sure I'm willing to absent myself from the relationship for months on end. I can live with a respectable place in the biz, but fame feels dangerous to the point of scaring me. Of course, someone like El Jay doesn't seem to be bothered by it, but the man knows how to pace himself.

Speaking of El Jay, he lets me know that the big reunion that was the topic of our meeting at the St. Francis, the day I met Lisa, is on and slotted for a world tour some time in the course of the next year. I can't believe it's actually happening—it's like the second best thing after the Beatles getting back together, except that it's real. It makes me think about the way Johnno went down, shot in the back like that... How fucking cowardly!

∞∞

It takes me some time to get into the studio frame of mind. Remembering the energy required to set up the place in Camden, I feel overwhelmed. I had more time then, mostly doing sessions in town and playing the clubs. But it's cool to have a place to pop in when the old muse kicks in.

I never mentioned Moose—a good buddy of mine from New York, who presently is *who knows where* in South America, doing business—but now isn't too late. I just received his call congratulating me on my wedding, and he mentioned that one of his friends—I shall call him Spork—a well-respected guitarist in a local band, is looking into building a studio in S.F., and that perhaps I should contact him.

I meet Spork down in the Mission. I immediately feel like it's not going to work, because the man isn't only taciturn, he also acts like he couldn't care less. I'm not in the habit of wasting my time, so I tell him it was nice meeting him, which honestly wasn't, but those are the things we say just because we're raised with a modicum of etiquette. But Spork warms up.

"How's Moose—still writing?"

"I'm sure he is—can't stop a writer from writing—but he's in Argentina right now."

"Yeah, he's got his hands in many baskets. So, I

hear you want to build a studio; you're in that famous English band, right? What do you have in mind, 16 tracks, maybe 24?"

"I just sold my London set-up, Helios, Studer, Fairchild comp, etcetera; yes, definitely 24 tracks."

"That's expensive gear, bud, so I guess you're aiming at building something similar?"

"Definitely, I plan on recording and mixing in the facility."

"Exactly where I'm at with the band—want to shop for location?"

Just like that, it all turns on a dime. I quickly discover that in spite of his demons, Spork's quite a nice guy—it's just a matter of getting used to his style.

The Mission and the South of Market are our best options as far as locations go. The Tenderloin is a contender, but I don't want to sit too close to Wally's studio on Hyde. The winds of change tell me that there's something going on in the South of Market that might jeopardize things in the long run. New construction is casting its long shadow across the warehouse districts and who knows where it might stop. It's not like we're buying a place, which could prove profitable if we were forced to move, but I don't have that kind of money right now, and neither does Spork. Perhaps it's something to consider before Hong Kong wealths start pouring in. I know I keep on repeating myself, but I will until some of my friends wake up to the inevitability of it. So, I repeat: buy a house in San Francisco before you can't afford one anymore!

And it's not just Hong Kong; it suffices to look towards Silicone Valley to realize something big is about to spread its wings. And even if I'm wrong, I don't thing San Francisco's about to become a ghost town any time soon. Now, I'm kind of forcing myself to walk my talk, aren't I? With the cost of equipment and construction added, how in the world are we gonna be able to come up with half a million bucks anyway?!

Spork laughs at the notion of buying instead of renting. He thinks I'm nuts. He's right since it's like banking on music being a reliable source of income. I mean, yes, the first two albums sold reasonably well and I'm still making good money from them, but they didn't yield fortunes. On top of it, the industry is fickle, and tastes change. Going with the trends may prove a worse idea than ignoring them, like selling out versus integrity. There's music, the art, and there's music, the business, which mustn't be confused. I think trend is more on the side of business than it is of art's. Music's a shapeshifter, while business is a hide-and-seek game full of posturing, ass-kissing, and back-stabbing. Music adapts—business either kills or dies. So, where does the musician stands? I tell you where the musician stands; she or he stands at the door of subtlety, making the slightest of adjustments in style without compromising the essence. He, or, she, or they, (for God's sake, can someone invent a proper pronoun!) make the changes their own. Take punk for instance; is Tom Petty's music punk rock? No fucking way—his promo co just said so—he never had to do anything but play what he loves to play! You know what

I'm saying, right? The only way to be called an innovator is to remain one's center at all times—ask El Jay. The man never changes—he's just a moody bloke whose style follows whatever inspires him, and many things do, from fast cars to the colors of culture. Trends never touch him, because he exists in the eye of change.

All this to say I don't know whether I'll be able to sustain a living with music or not, which also brings me to thinking that investing such large amounts of dough in a studio may not be the smartest of ideas—exactly Spork's point. So, buying is out.

The fact that gear is easy to come by and falling in price is indicative something's wrong somewhere. It looks like commercial studios are taking a hit and I can't quite put my finger on the reasons. Spork says that we're the reason, that more and more artists are building their own so that they don't have to spend insane fortunes in recording fees. He also says, in no uncertain terms, that musicians being such narcissistic sons of bitches, they think they can be just as good producers as the best of them. I don't totally disagree, but I've also come across producers afflicted with similar stigmas, to the point of thinking they can outdo the players. In the end, it has nothing to do with musicians or producers, but human nature—some of us are born saints, others, real motherfuckers—that's just the gist of it. The fact remains that more and more mid-size to big studios are closing.

Spork and I conclude that the idea of a commercial facility is downright unrealistic and that building one for the fun of it is the only way to go. After all, we only need to record our respective bands, which might end up being as much as we can accommodate.

We find a suitable place on Treat, in the Mission, a small warehouse with a vacant apartment on top that goes for a reasonable rent. The owner, Guillermo, is a nice old chap who plays in a Mariachi band with the dad of one of our local guitar heroes. It's a small world, thinking of it.

So, Spork and I are set—it's just a matter of getting a team in there to build the rooms. Of course, someone needs to design the place first, and since I've done it with the studio in London, I've got a good idea on how to go at it.

It's not like we're in business, Spork and I, but we sign papers anyway because we both think alike when it comes down to rationale. Why take chances when you can exist on the safe side for just a small lawyer's fee? In the end it's a pie sliced straight in the middle—a 50/50 no-nonsense deal. Just for the fun of it, we name the studio *The Cube* because that's what the main room looked like before we hung the acoustic panels.

Sadly, I couldn't find a Helios board, but I love the api; it's a beaut with plenty of sparkle. Otherwise, same Studer, Scully, and plate reverb, with tons of great outboard gear. Spork and I are happy campers!

Lisa and Spork's wife, Roxy, did a great job taking care of the decor and smudging the place. The back of the control room has the feel of a Turkish den sans the nargiles. You just plop your bode on thick cushions, let yourself be returned to the womb, and may the music take you to the source of your dreams. It's possible the Goddesses overdid it, but they're part of it as much as we are. We're all having fun here, aided by some Humboldt green and a few *Anchor Steams*!

All is calibrated and ready to go. Spork's band will be in next week with me at the faders. Can't wait for it—*The Cube* awaits!

Funny how things can change so quickly! It turns out that Ric the drummer can't make it because something big happened, but Spork's ace percussionist, Breeze King, volunteers to sit on our next album. I love Breeze—a total prince of a guy!

So far, all is good in San Francisco. I made the right choice, but I can't say I don't miss London—I left part of my heart there by selling the Camden House. Mind you, I still have two rentals there, one Lisa and I could easily turn into our place. Actually, the more I think about it, the more it makes sense. Since I'm now permanently based in the States—it would be great to keep an anchor there, if only for the sake of not falling into hopeless nostalgia. Plus, I like to visit El Jay's country pad on occasion and jam at the old free house.

Lisa was actually wondering how I fared having been replanted in new soil. She seems relieved by the idea, something to do with not being responsible for my uprooting. That's how this incredible woman thinks—she cares like no-one I have ever met anywhere, not even in my imagination. You can't truly grasp the nature of people not from this world until you become associated with one of them; the sheer alienness of uncompromised authenticity through love is a gift from the cosmos that can never be taken for granted. It's the stuff that needs to be revered with every dawn awakening, every moment of lucidity, every bit of courageous thinking. It is the love that is unconditionally returned with matching kindness, never before and never after the right time. One naturally knows when it's here.

14 – THE HEALING

Spork's band hits the charts at the same time our third album makes its entry into the Billboard. Breeze can't believe he's on parallel "climbers." We drink to the occasion with plans to tour together. Ric's back in the fold, so all is right with the world!

Spork's band is on MTV—the two are a perfect fit. Personally, I prefer to stay clear off it. I know it's reckless not to take advantage of the medium, but I want to be able to walk the streets of San Francisco with Lisa without having to say hi to everybody. As much as I think it's cool to be popular in both love and hate, I abhor idolatry. It's different in the context of my work, where being recognized for achievements is a necessary process of validation that keeps one on the creative track, but I set the limits at the public level. I wish, as much as the next guy, to keep my privacy intact. One may say that losing that privilege comes with the territory, but I disagree. I'm not saying it's the public's fault, rather, it's the responsibility of the artist to set the boundaries, and one of them is to not flirt with MTV. Mind you, Spork stays in the background, knowing damn well the singer can't get enough of the spotlight, so, just like me; he's still able to go outside like normal people do.

I'm not denying Spork and I occasionally get accosted by the observant soul, but it's like meeting a friend on the street, it's brief and everyone goes on happy with their business. That level of recognition suits me; it's paced, it flows in perfect time with life, it's the one that makes me appreciate humankind without ever having to recourse to thinking about whether they're decent people or not. I was on Oxford Street with El Jay once, and even though folks were cognizant of space and privacy, it was hard to have so many eyes on us. El Jay was comfortable ignoring the gazes, but frankly, it embarrassed me. It's kind of funny since I don't have that problem performing. It's probably because I've accepted the stage as a place dedicated to the purpose of extreme visibility.

At this point, I'm wondering where to go with life's report. I see technical points and band shenanigans as devoid of substance—although I deem them necessary items of orientation—that being said, I seek balance. After all, I'm the one reading and rereading the lines, and the last thing I need, right now, is fall to the plodding mundanity of my own words. It's a rash, and perhaps unfair, assessment of the self in regard to memory, but there's no reason to go on with artifacts of little consequence. Then again, it might be nothing more than a matter of perspective.

In truth, the writing could add up to being a book, but one never knows. It's tricky to awaken to one's own slice of reality, sensing that sitting on the reflection may be the worse thing that can happen to consciousness. Life's paradox culminates in a dilemma when it comes to pulling one's thoughts out of one's arse.

But there's a form of subliminal method to the madness. This self-indulging pause puts me in touch with the emotional side of my thinking; the doubts that link with deep-rooted insecurities, intellectual elation with a sense of need, competitiveness with the void of incompletion, etc... Everything can become a marker to the observant mind, and right now, I come to realize that in spite of the successes, the financial self-sufficiency, the love in my life, my many friends... I'm not sure I'm as happy as I claim to be. There is an eroding to the lining of my core being that feels of apprehensive rawness, a longing for things on the brink of being forever gone; it's akin to the past knocking at the door, like the five year old tumbling down the street, only to meet death in the eyes, when those same eyes are my own from this very present. It's an existential mash-up of all that's left unchecked, now rising in an ominous ferment. I become the sum of all the nows that find no resolve—the past and future ones. I am being called to the vortex of the neglected, the unjustly abandoned—hands desperately clutching at sanity to feed and momentarily sate the depths of dementia. I could go on... The fact is that I don't feel so well inside.

Lisa's intuitions don't lie. She's no fool to those who feign happiness even when they have no reason to be unhappy. It's not like I want to hide how I feel—I don't know what I feel! But regardless, she cuts through the layers to get right to the point.

"Is there something bothering you?"

I'm not going to play Mr. Unreachable—it's a guy trick that comes at too high a cost—so, I try to explain in my best universal language, also known as sincerity, what's up with me. But Lisa's not one to waste time listening when too much has already been said in loops. She interrupts letting me know I'm not allowing her to help me. How dares she?! But she's right—I'm unconsciously pretending openness while holding to the reins of control, rationalizing on reasons, excuses, failing at taking responsibility for the emotional mess I'm in, not surrendering to the reality that my bruised soul is in dire need of self-love. I give up. I sob like a child—the one that lives within.

Lisa's a natural psychic healer on top of being a glorious masseuse and an astrologer. I understand *psychic* is a dirty word among the rational of mind, but I think it's unfair, considering the immeasurable amount of unknown below the superficial layers of the physical. I'm not purveying to the crystal ball or tarot card reader dames of common folklore, although I'm quite fond of the decorum, but rather to genuine connectivity with the deeper strata of natural knowledge. If one understands that it doesn't take science for the body to put a foot in front of the other, or react with stealth to obstacles and danger, one knows what I'm talking about. None of this means that I cognize the precise metrics of what makes things tick, but my mind is awake to the knowledge that we tend to hide a lot of readily available and invaluable information from ourselves. It's a solid start in my book. But Lisa beats me to it because she lives it instead of rationalizing about it like I do. So, when she offers to do a psychic healing, I surrender to it being a good way to get to the bottom of the churning, but not without flexing a bit of personal mentalism—what guys do to show off, and also the stuff that has brought me to the gates of my own control issues—something I'm sure Lisa has a medicine for, providing that I can relax enough to let her do her job. Don't we love the brain!

The child is the issue, or rather; the child, in his arrested developmental state, is the issue. As I grew to become the adult, a big part of my early troubles have remained in the form of a young *aspect personality* awaiting its turn to be redeemed. How do I know that? Well, let me put it this way; I take chances with my thinking, or, more simply, I let my imagination loose on the emotional trail. What said imagination tells me is for the observer to decipher—that's roughly how it works. So, the child cries for the love his parents robbed him of, and on he waits for something that will never come. That's when Lisa moves in with her take on missing love, and the answer is, yes: self-love. Nothing to do with narcissism or indulging in the ritual of jacking off, as some of my slow-witted friends allude to, but all to do with the daily practice of self-respect, of recognizing achievements over failures, of thanking the body for the bloody hard work, mainly by cutting down on the junk and exercising more, etc... You know what she means! It's not as simple as it seems, since it takes letting the child do the talking without the mind messing things up. In other words, channel the child and the pain while keeping the shields up, because you're no longer the child—get it? That's the gist of it. I'm all for it because I'm ready to let the kid go; and if mom and dad haven't been there to do their job, then I'm going to have to be the one providing the love—by first loving myself, that is. It's like bringing two far-apart *present points* together—in essence, the kind of work that defines the principles of psychic healing.

Now, Lisa can't work alone with this, because the true healer is the self. It goes by the maxim that no-one gets healed that doesn't want to heal themselves. It takes two to tango. She's the channel that conducts pure, universal energy to the recipient, while the latter opens the gates to allow for it to flow in and free the ills groundward.

I'm not talking about flushing the child, of course, but the pain within the child rather. When gone, the kid will resume with his growth, reverting to being one of the many memories of my youth, the benign aspects of time fleeting about, occasionally landing on a thought in whatever present.

Since everything takes a modicum of effort before manifesting in something useful, the same goes with personal healing. The effort, in this case, is to cognize on the value of bringing all pertinent elements together. Even though the parents can't make it, for one Father's dead, and two, Mother's rather self-involved with similar issues, I've got to play their parts through the process of self-love. But things being what they are, it won't work if I don't forgive first. I can't go on saying *good riddance!* without engaging in the process of sabotage towards making myself healthier in body and mind. Anger, as justified as it may be, is of no use.

It becomes interesting when, at the beginning of a séance, Lisa mentions Father being around. I'm not totally surprised by it, which is good, and even more so since I don't feel emotionally stimulated by the news. And here he is; I can see him now. He's dressed in a beige trench coat and matching fedora. He's now a private investigator—a regular Sam Spade—on a break from his assignment. I ask how he's doing.

"Things are good."

He seems happy in a serious kind of way, doing what he always wanted to do. He moved out of reading noir novels to becoming a character within them, except this one includes me as well.

I come out of my reverie. It's not happening—it's just the recollection of a dream I had not so long ago.

Lisa asks me if it's OK for him to stick around—I'm fine with it. Then, as if she could see him, she asks him if English is OK—English's OK.

Since when does he speak English? Apparently, he does, according to his message:

"I totally screwed up; I'm deeply sorry!"

I don't see or hear him, but I feel like hugging him. It wasn't so hard, was it?!

OK, now I see him! He's standing by the woodpile, outside a house in the Northern California mountains, a place of odd familiarity, as if seen from the eyes of a faraway self—I talk to him, aware I've been having these conversations for decades. Things become strange when time and space decide to go by other rules.

The amazing thing is that all anger towards him is gone instantly. The past doesn't change, but my appreciation of it is radically altered. I don't even bother feeling suspicious about the sudden healing—it is what it is and I don't see how anything would veer from it—it is done with and irreversible!

I shall keep this short. I manage, taking advantage of a business meeting in London, to hop over to Eastern France to say hi to Mother.

While in the back of the car that takes us to Father's grave, I put my arm around her shoulders. I expect her to recoil, but instead, she gets closer, resting her head against my upper arm. I comb her cropped hair with my fingers, showing the kind of affection towards her that I had always wanted to express. I realize how much I had craved to tell her how much I loved her, so I tell her I love her and she tells me she loves me. We both cry. I am now Father and she is Child. I don't mind; I'm old enough for that and the child within is now free to play—he is loved as well.

15 – THE TWINS & MOOSE

I'll start with a date: July 1st 1985. Lisa's within a couple of weeks of delivering twins. That's all we know, twins—no gender. We took the natural birth classes, so we and the midwife are ready for the big date.

The last two years have been busy in a good way. *The Cube* is still going strong, but there have been changes on the business front. While Spork's band is going through changes in the form of various growing and *ungrowing* pains, Herbie, Andy, Ric, and I called it quits after the release of the fourth album, at which point the label let us go, allowing me to get re-signed as a solo artist with a bit of help from El Jay. It frees me from having to make circles around schedules or being forced to impose my owns. Even though Lisa and I visit Britain, and now France, with predictable regularity, it's never with the pressures of the past. I've reduced the touring to evenly spaced dates, putting bands together on-demand rather than committing to complex and often problematic relationships. It is true that the music industry is kind of in shambles, like bands being dropped at the peak of success while owing all kinds of back monies to the label. Spork's an authority on the subject. It's like the rats are taking over the ship ahead of the unavoidable act of having to leave it. Think mismanagement at a global level—probably why synths are killing the guitar, but that's mostly bad rap from the rags.

In other words, things call for a realignment of the thinking process, but I just call it good timing, since Lisa and I are about to become parents and I need to take a leave of absence from the job—a good excuse to get into songwriting, as well as plain writing. Yes, something's mounting and I intend on tapping its resources before it recedes into forgetfulness.

After a fairly long labor, the twins are born on Monday, July 22nd; first, Muse, a girl, at 2:31 p.m., and then, Wind, a boy, at 2:44—one a Cancer, the other a Leo. Lisa and I had spoken of the possibility, but never seriously due to the near-implausibility of it happening. And then, bam! This kind of synchronicity is what lets me know when things are meant to be. Lisa is tired but beaming with joy. She looks healthy though, and beyond some minor tearing, she's now pain-free. The boy had to be turned around, but it was the whole extent of the scare. Both babies are healthy and presently sleeping on my chest, while Lisa is being sewn back together—but I jest.

I doesn't take long for the twins to develop distinct personalities; and are we in for some action! They are both gorgeous; Muse with her big, brown eyes, and Wind with green-blue ones, like Mother. Lisa and I are in love with a double serving of miraculous, two souls gracing our lives with their immeasurable company. We agree they're not our creations, simply that we biologically and spiritually channeled them onward to the physical. Of course, and in all fairness, Lisa did the brunt work like all women do, but we're not here to split hair.

Naturally, taking care of two newborns is immensely exhausting, and tempers get frayed. But we soldier on, incrementally getting more efficient and less panicked when things don't go right. I don't have to tell anyone about the obvious, only one thing though, and it has a lot to do with the way my parents raised me: regardless of how one might end up being frustrated, love has to remain the main theme of the deal. I know it's not always the case from what transpires, but I insist that there isn't a single reason to get mad at your kids for being what they are. Just take a deep breath and move on with the love.

When I'm not home doing my share, I'm in *The Cube* laying tracks with Breeze who's taken a liking to the place. Most of my other work, meaning sitting in at sessions, is primarily done at the Plant, or at Lucas's place, up in the Marin hills. I often bring Lisa and the twins to these gigs, where they're always treated like royalty. I can't complain about how things are doing, and I make sure that every morning, when I look out the windows from our nest on Telegraph Hill, and I see the Bridge and the Marin Headlands, a prayer full of thanks is sent onwards with all intent to make the world a better place. I mean it, because I never take anything for granted. Knowing where I belong makes me a happier human!

Since it's not forbidden to combine business with pleasure, when one of my friends in London invites me to sit on his latest album, I take the opportunity to introduce the twins to Mother. She doesn't know what to do with them, anymore than she knew what to do with us back when, but it makes her happy all the same. Can't put a woman down for her sufferings!

Back in London, we stay at the house we converted into our second home a few years back. We get together with Neil, Fuzzy, Chrissie, and Zack who came with Chrissie at our wedding, and the couples' little ones, one each, a girl and boy of similar age as the twins. It's a total racket of screaming, banging, out-shouting one another, but it's the most fun we've had since we've known each other. I also invited El Jay and his girlfriend, but he canceled on pretext that a race had cumulated into an unending argument about this and that. We'll inevitably catch up as we always do.

Out of the blue, I get a call from Moose, who happens to be in London on business with his lovely wife and his two kids. Just as I wonder how he got the house's new number, he tells me that he rang Herbie and Jenny first; that's how the laws of connectivity work—in precise sequentiality. It's the way it goes with Moose, like he knows things before they happen. I don't call him my brother of a different mother for nothing.

One may wonder why Moose hasn't been mentioned more often if we're that close. One answer could be that I respect his privacy, another, that I feel his name might make some business sorts nervous if they heard that I knew him personally. No-one lives in a vacuum around Moose, although, I can ascertain that he's not the type to rat on his enemies. The man has too much class for that. Anyway, what I'm getting at is that until this point there was no good reason to talk about him. OK to leave it at that?

So Moose, besides us chatting about the latest, has matters he would like to discuss in private. We set up a date for a week down the road, in San Francisco.

I had a great time working on the album, getting to reconnect with old acquaintances and meeting new friends. I like flow without the proverbial, conditional damming—we pass through life, not get snagged by it like going through bramble. I like smooth. I get my kicks out of things working as they should—when everyone does their job to the best of their abilities. It's amazing how well gears mesh around efficient, responsible folks; what's not is when a vast demography resorts to chaos, even though they tend to bitch about it—to each their own. But I digress.

I did my parts for free. It sounds crazy to travel half-way around the world to do some guy a favor, but you know what's crazier? It's to not heed the rule of returns. The man's a good friend strapped for cash, who can't afford an unknown studio cat, but could definitely get a boost by having a few house names behind him. Just common courtesy, especially when I was once in his shoes and El Jay was there for me. What goes around, comes around—always does.

It's not like I'm rolling in dough. Things are getting tight. There are bands and solo artists popping up everywhere, demanding their slice of the pie, some deserving, some not, but all the same, and the pie isn't getting any bigger. It's not just the greed on top and the art-starved bean counters working for them that are creating the mess, it's the sheer proliferation of middlemen pushing their latest talent on the market, one one-hit wonder at a time. I could be exaggerating, but it sure looks that way. Sorry for showing discontentment that doesn't belong here—it's not part of the flow I often speak of, and happiness isn't built on that kind of foundation anyway, so forgive me if I err on the side of apprehension here and there.

With the twins getting bigger and the lower income—the fourth album not having sold so well—my mind is looking for options. My Hong Kong theory is pushing me in the direction of investing in real estate, and I'm duly considering following the tip. I'm contemplating the avenues, both the Richmond and the Sunset, as being the big winners on the residential market, with the hottest zones closer to the downtown, but I see promise to the west, all the way to the Pacific. There's also a future for the South of Market, but it's riskier and out of my league; I'll leave it to developers and the big banks behind them.

Moose comes over the house—his first time—the day after we return from London.

"Nice place you have here, mate!"
"Thanks, brother; Lisa found it as you know, and of course, her artistic touch is what brings it together!"

"Hi Lis, how have you been?"

"Well, Moose, but with the twins, I haven't had much time to think about myself. How's the family doing?"

"The kids are growing up and Kay's the exemplary mother, as you already know; so all's well. Of course, she says hi!"

"So, they didn't follow you here?"

"Nope, they flew straight out of London to Buenos Aires—things to take care of at the ranch."

"Well, please, make yourself at home. Why don't you fire up that joint on the coffee table!"

The point of Moose's visit is to tempt me with a business deal I can't refuse—the way he sees it, of course, but Lisa and I are all ears.

"I'm not blind, mate, you're not exactly cut for the whole superstar bullshit, even though there's a place for you up there, but I don't think it's where your heart wants to go; am I wrong? Also, any sober man with an eye can see where things are going with the industry; it's more cutthroat than it's ever been and styles are moving away from where you're at. You're no El Jay with his own edifice—you were born too late for that. But I don't want to rattle your house, that's not what I'm here for; ultimately you make your choices, and you know me, I like being wrong when it serves my friends. But let me cut to the chase. If you've been able to survive comfortably in this business for all this time, it's because you have a mind capable of recognizing wind direction and boundaries. You've mentioned Hong Kong on a number of occasions, and since I work with the place, as well as its neighbors, I couldn't agree more with you on where the money is about to go. You've got that sussed out, brother! What I'm getting at is that I could use a mind like yours in my business—I'm offering a partnership, no questions asked. You don't necessarily have to live in Argentina, but you two and the twins might have to spend some time down there, just because you'd be silly not to. You think about it, guys, but I would really like you with me on this; and I promise, the music will only suffer minimally."

I'm stumped; what can I say?! My mind makes circles around the offer like a wild thing wondering what has just fallen from the sky. I mean, Moose is in the tea trade, something besides my taste for a few varietals, I know nothing about.

"Hey, didn't you tell me once that you studied freighting and economics in senior high or college? Is that too much coming around to bite you? I understand—you've told me your story—but those are serious assets you don't have to throw away quite yet."

Yes, I told Moose about the misbegotten classes—more than I care to remember about. But what's in freighting that doesn't involve endless, boring paperwork? Economics, well, unless you're a financier, the rest is common sense—balance the books and you're good to go—still, more paperwork!

"Forget the paperwork, that's the office's job, I'm talking about meeting people, creating contacts, knowing how to deal with the various bureaucracies around the globe, meaning—depending on the country—individuals ranging from unflappable to full-out corruptible. Doesn't that sound like fun to you? Of course, you've got to educate yourself around tariffs, most of them originating from the colonial days."

"But Moose, what makes you think I would be interested in working in commerce?"

"Because I know by just knowing you that you're presently contemplating survival options, because if you were not, you wouldn't be you. Who in the world buys four houses and a recording studio instead of snorting coke and banging prostitutes out of their first royalty money? So, yes, I could be wrong, but how are you going to buy real estate in San Francisco—because I know that's what you're thinking of doing—if you don't have the cash? I'm offering you that option, mate!"

"And what's in it for you?"

"Having you, Lis, and the kids around, that's what I'm counting on."

"What about you, Lisa?"

"As long as my base remains in San Francisco, I don't mind traveling. I'm like Moose, I like the idea of an extended family."

I'm not committing quite yet, *mais les jeux sont pratiquement fait*. No need to translate.

16 – CULTURES & CUSTOMS

Just like the previous chapter, let's start with a date, like today's, October 16th 1989, and wiggle our way back from here.

The twins, Muse and Wind, are now over four years old. What a treat to see them at this age, developmentally on track, but also very much in charge of that particular kind of knowledge us adults seem to have lost along the road of learning the things all generations are forced to assimilate. This thought alone makes me nervous, because as you know, what I was told was mostly that the world was a hopeless, miserable place no-one in their right mind would want to live in. So, I'm all in favor of children's miracle thinking and never-ending explorations of the impossible without interference from grownup cynicism.

Being a strong proponent of *we're born with access to an immense pool of knowledge*, I see brilliance channeled through my kids in such obvious ways that it chagrins me to observe similar brilliance being stratified into calcified zones of submissiveness by poor parenting. I'm not saying that Lisa and I are experts at it, only that we can recognize there's far greater awareness behind those eyes than the world cares to look into. It helps that we both are curious souls, and perhaps it's what allows us to be artistes in the first place. In delicious irony, irony itself is what may have prevented me from falling into the clutches of cynicism, the kind that negates hope in the self and competes with the joy of others to the point of seeking their emotional collapse.

That was what my parents wished of me and my sisters, even if they were incapable of recognizing the systematic abuse that was used to quench that unconscious thirst, the kind as it was, borne of what one may call *generational trauma.*

Perhaps, by being subjected to such out of control vindictiveness was I made immune to those family and collective curses. But I suspect it took a lot of work and even courage on my part as well as Lisa's, having herself been subjected to abuse—although a very different kind much harder to diagnose—before we could let go of the stigma through much proverbial skin-shedding. In other words, over our dead bodies are our progeny to be taken down those ill-fated historical lanes.

We still live in our colorful house on Telegraph Hill. It's tight, but a tight home keeps hearts warm and love in check. OK, we live in a beautiful place, so, following the analogy, life might be quite different in a trailer park shack on wheels; still, the coldness of a large colonial house, beautiful or not, may not inspire love to stick around—just saying.

We did buy property in both the Sunset and the Richmond, but later on that.

Right now, I'm finalizing the paperwork with Spork—he's buying me out, having deemed that his band needed its own place, as in without me around. It's not like I'm being sacked, to the contrary—it's an amicable arrangement that profits us both, since one of the aforementioned properties on 20th and Irving is about to become my very personal studio. Well, personal only to the extent that I'm the sole proprietor, since a big, local household name is courting me to let him use the facility for his next album.

I understand the readership (if it were to ever be more than a virtual element in all of this,) might want to know why I don't just name the guy—or all the others for that matter, including me. Simply that it would revert my original intent of writing about life's emotional qualitative to mere biographically-based, name-dropping factoids of no value to me. As I've said, I abhor idolatry. To name anyone God, lest this becomes the one innuendo that breaks the rule, is the apogee of the dysfunctional way of thinking that plagues the field. Why in the world do we put rockers, dictators, and religious leaders on such unreachable platforms, when the guys eat, shit, and stink like everyone else? Please, people, validate talent and charisma, but refrain from making an embarrassment of yourself! If you go to a concert and are having fun, dance with the person next to you, or share a joint, or whatever, but don't give yourself to someone who's having their personal fun up on that stage—it's everyone's time to honor the moment equally. Fame is nothing but the stroking of egos and the fanning of the flames of narcissism. You're just giving an excuse to a perfectly regular human to think they're something greater than themselves—it's a lie. I rest my case!

Let's return to the deal with Moose. Yes, it's about tea and the world of trading in commodities, but it's substantially more. Moose, as it must be stressed, is an accomplished, multitalented musician, just as comfortable on drums and bass as he is on horns. So, one must understand that getting into business with him, is in some respect an extension of what I've always done. Let it be also said that we both share views on what was just written in the previous paragraph. It thus explains why, just as Moose said, it was a deal I couldn't refuse. And yes, the income allowed me to put down-payments on a few residences in San Francisco, which inspired him to do the same. But I suspect that he already had it all lined up before we even talked about it, because it wouldn't have been Moose otherwise. The man has been known before for having been a step ahead!

As promised, I met numerous characters through my new job; but in spite of all the folklore, the posturing, and the standoffs, I have mostly come across interesting individuals and made quite a few friends. World trade is a cultural reality that requires a keen understanding of customs, and above all, the pressure points of the human ego. Always acknowledge your place as a guest when visiting, and exercise polite, confident firmness when visited. It's amazing what a bit of well-paced etiquette can do in tricky situations, without having to compromise one's integrity. It doesn't cost anything, and may bring rewards. Can you spell win-win?

Of course, those are difficult times when a shipment sits in the stagnant air of a steamy port hangar because the local guerrillas have taken over, or the longshoremen are striking, or some harlequinesque administrator is clogging the pipes of commonsense— generally the recipe for catastrophe in tea vernacular—

times that must be made the shortest possible with the help of those you have graced with your respect and reliable kindness. I'm not talking about flattery here, but the manner by which one, after having understood their place in the realm of communication, go on to deploy the methods by which cargos travel the shortest and fastest routes. It's the nature of the trade and nothing else will do. Everything I know, I learned from Moose, who's always been kind enough to trust me with my first steps.

All revolves around the human connection, the proximate one as much as the by-proxy one; neither of which can exist without backbone, clarity, and vision.

I mentioned earlier that after having completed our quota with the label, Herbie, Andy, Ric, and I got let go and I was re-signed as a solo artist. So, following poor promo and, predictably, bad sales of my next two LPs, both instrumental, Jenny informed me that it was time to part with the big boys, which I took as carte blanche to fly my wings with my own label, *Criminal Records*, conjunct to a distribution deal with El Jay's company. Somehow, I felt free. Yes, it's like a relationship with a real human; things can sour up to the point of oppressiveness. Jenny's a nice enough gal, but she's all business, and even more so now that Herbie has left her to go back to the UK and never be heard of again. No-one I know there has seen him, and it's rumored he might even have returned to South Africa, whence he came originally. All Jenny could say in regard to my situation with the label was, "Things are tough, dude, nothing I can do about it." Well, yes, there's that, but truly, she was no longer interested. In other words, my music had aged and the bloody synths had taken over. But I jest.

I'm not totally surprised to find other rockers in the tea business, though I must say they seem peripheral compared to Moose and I. As superficial as their roles may be, it's evident that we're not the only ones who've looked to other avenues for financial stability. Let's face it, there's a shelf life to everything and the music business is particularly vulnerable to the perishability of what it deems relevant. So, finding our kin amid blowfish farms in Scotland, or opening brew pubs in Northern California and Portland, Oregon, shouldn't come as lateral novelty. I mean, how many studio cats, myself included, haven't profited from jingles? Does anyone truly believe that bringing one's talent to the level of sucking up to a corporation's ludicrous idea that consumers are mere reflexive numbers is anything other than business? OK, a bit harsh, but you get the point. All this to say that even some of the megastars have built cushions for themselves, because who knows what could happen in the foreseeable future if music were to fall to the level of mere background noise. We're lucky that passions have brought our art to the rooms of dedicated listeners, and I'm sure, those places aren't about to disappear anytime soon, but I always think in terms of the potential for major shifts to happen in the human psyche—it's all in the realm of understanding how history repeats itself with amendments to suit the times.

Of course, the true heroes are those who stick to the arts and never let go regardless of the risk of ending up broke. I admire their trust in the present and fearlessness of the future—somehow, they always manage.

I'm not sure where this brain of mine is trying to go with this, but let's assume that it has to say what it deems must be said, if for the sake of preventing the festering of whatever cluster of useless beliefs in the backroom. But one thing is certain—and let that be the savior to my sanity—this brain knows that it's strictly addressing an imaginary audience. How comforting it is to be in the company of trusted friends!

So, yes, Moose and I love music as much as the next person and it goes without saying that we manage to lay tracks in a friend's sixteen-track studio in Buenos Aires, a funky Neve console teamed to an antiquated 3M recorder with a few bad calibration cards, and a mic locker full of banged up U67s, C 12s, and Coles Type A's. That doesn't stop us from having fun; on the contrary, the ambience is right on track with the music. It's like operating from an illegal facility with the rale of a lone tenor sax playing the score in the smoky background.

Lisa, Kay, and the kids are in charge of the cover, and man, what a loving process that is! And thus, with the help of some talent from the plantation, we record the first *Criminal* album titled *Late Night Noises*, which we have pressed in L.A. and distributed by El Jay's label. It's not a romper, but it's far from light on substance. As to its success, well, since we threw caution to the wind, we don't expect to make a fortune out of it—but fun's the reward, remember?

Somehow, a couple of the tunes make it to the local radio, prompting a wink in my direction from across the office where Moose has his station.

"Hey, mate, we're stars in our own little part of the world; what about that!"

I feel like saying that with some promo we could break those boundaries, but I refrain knowing too well Moose isn't too keen on exposure at the mo.

Lisa, the twins, and I, spend our time alternating between Argentina, London, and San Francisco. And though it sounds like a lot of constant uprooting, it's not as complicated or scary as it may appear at first, especially since Muse and Wind are young enough to spare us the ordeal of bouncing between schools and home schooling. For now, it's a world of discovery that stands before them, and I must admit, us adults, as well.

Lisa is taking classes at Psychic Horizon in San Francisco on her way to being ordained as a Reverend, while I try to hold to my seat at the various Bay Area studios and comprehend where my recent interest in quantum physics is taking me.

On the subject of quantum mechanics, I'm a little bit at a loss as to why all these brilliant thinkers are not equating the evasiveness of waves, particles, sensors, etc, at being defined by traditional tools of observation, to choices and beliefs on the part of the observer. Since the tools and the observer themselves are made of the same stuff as the object being analyzed, doesn't it make sense to introduce the notion of units of consciousness filtered by the colored lenses of individual and mass belief systems having something to do with it? What about projecting reality as opposed to receiving it, as it is commonly accepted? I mean, we go on saying things like *I create my own reality* without really believing that we do. Imagine for an instant that instead of observing those waves and particles, we created them—and I mean literally, and not necessarily from the standpoint of the physical—wouldn't those wave, particles, sensors, and whatever objects of reference and interference in all of their probabilities take on a different meaning if awareness and purpose were attached to them? I'm just saying this, *waves exist as particles at the threshold of consciousness, otherwise they don't exist at all*, but I'm neither a scientist nor a philosopher. I'll leave it at that.

17 – THE BIG ONE

I'm on the Golden Gate Bridge, returning from Lucas' place, when the thing starts swinging wildly to the point the Z32 can barely stay on its lane. I know it's a big one by the way the cables and the deck don't seem to know which direction to take, now that they have been jolted out of their static state. It lasts the eternity of something like fifteen seconds, but I know it's that long. By the time it ends, the traffic is at a standstill, but luckily enough, I've made it close enough to the toll booths that I'm able to sneak onto the Presidio lane and get out of there. My thoughts are on my family, especially now that the radio is broadcasting from Candlestick Park where the World Series between San Francisco and Oakland is happening. The guy's talking about structural damage to parts of the stadium, and just then, it dawns on me that some serious shit has hit the city. Every access to the Marina is blocked by traffic, and there's smoke coming from numerous places in the district. I have to make my way west before I can come around again eastward on Jackson Street towards downtown. What a mess! None of the lights are working and everyone's on the streets; in the distance, the green firework of exploding transformers, all the way across the Bay, brings on the ominous winds of catastrophe. My heart beats in a frenzy, which is the worse thing that can happen when driving a sports car; thence I calm down by assuring myself that things are alright and that getting into a fender bender isn't going to get me closer to my loved ones. It takes me an hour to reach Greenwich Street and park at the bottom of the public stairs that go to my house. To my distress, Lisa and the twins are out, so I decide to run the distance to the Marina where Nonna lives. It's not exactly next door, but I make it in record time, ignoring the burning in my chest and the blood rushing through my system at the beat of an insane tune. On my way, I come across police, ambulances, and fire trucks surrounding entire rows of collapsed apartment buildings; it smells heavily of gas and sewer out of cracks in the asphalt. It's becoming difficult to run in between the clusters of rubber-neckers, and rescue and service personnel, but I'm nearly there. Thank God, the house is still upright and sure enough, Lisa, Nonna, Muse, and Wind are standing on the sidewalk with a group of neighbors. When I get there, I'm dripping with sweat. Lisa's in tears from relief at the sorry sight of me, and the kids are screaming with joy and excitement. Nonna is her regular stoic self, but I can tell she's also relieved. She asks us in for a glass of wine.

We drive back to Telegraph Hill in Lisa's car. I'm somewhat apprehensive about not having checked for gas leaks when I first got there, but everything's fine aside from the crooked wall pictures and some broken china. The Deluxe still stands proud; unfortunately the Balladeer lies on the floor with a snapped head—but it's only a fucking guitar. In the scope of all the things that could have gone wrong, we can consider ourselves lucky. Tomorrow, I'll check on the rest of my gear, which is in storage in Marin at the cartage company.

In the meantime there is some serious shit going on outside, as it turns out some sections of the upper freeways in both San Francisco and Oakland have collapsed on the lower traffic and I fear the worst for whoever's buried there under tons of concrete. A chunk of the upper Bay Bridge has also fallen onto the lanes below and it's rumored some vehicles have plunged into the bay's frigid waters. It's considered a miracle that there was substantially less traffic on the roads because of the World Series—I can't fathom what would have happened on a regular day. Now that I've found my bearings, holy crap, what a fucking scare that was! I swear I thought the Golden Gate was going to come loose and hit the brine!

I'm not going to go over the details of the damage and what the quake did to the hearts of the people. I had been through a couple of heavy shakes previously, but this one was the one that made all of us come to face the fragility of our lives and the precariousness of the ground on which we stand. We never realize what others go through when it happens beyond the line of sight, but suffice to say, when one knows the traumas associated with catastrophes such as war, one never forgets. I can't bear thinking about the horrors of conflict, and the dehumanization that goes around war rhetorics when those at ground zero have to live in terror and the despair of loss. Motherfucker!

We exist without electricity for a couple of days, but we enjoy the life around candles and the simplicity that comes when things don't need to happen. We go out on walks during the day and play card games in the evening after wholesome dinners from the pantry supplies. Time is irrelevant when your mortality sits close by—one becomes humble, almost graceful, and definitely appreciative of the little time allotted to this precious life. Before going to bed, we gather in a circle and sing songs, mostly on the twins' request.

It's with a heavy heart that I learn the car of one of my good buddies was found crushed between the upper and lower decks of the Nimitz in Oakland. He was returning from the airport after a visit with his family in New York when the quake happened. The event touches me like it touches everyone else in the Bay Area—one way or the other, no-one is spared.

I very much doubt any soul that has gone through the Loma Prieta earthquake will ever forget.

18 – TEA & JUNGLE NOISES

The quake's a good reason to spend some time in London. Not that we don't want to stick around, mind you, but we'd like to get the twins out of here, because whichever way you shake it, they got traumatized by the whole thing. Too much, too close, and too fast equals massive sensory overload for four year old kids. I guess we're acting like privileged brats compared to those who have to stick around without a home, but I've always been of the belief that caring about family comes first—not doing so is simply unreal. After the dust settles, we'll check things out before flying to Buenos Aires and rejoin Moose and the gang.

I can't believe how much London has changed since the mid-seventies, when parts of Camden were crawling with squatters. I'm not sure whether the EU is responsible for the new wealth or not, but needless to say that since joining, the city has gone through a major overhaul. I can't even recognize Covent Garden—there's this huge Bank sitting its big ass where a razed neighborhood once lived, and my old, decrepit apartment, before I bought the Camden houses, is now a posh dwelling for the well-to-do. But why should I resist change when it brings me fortunes, I mean, the two homes are now worth so much money that I almost feel embarrassed talking about owning property in the City, and yet, prices keep on climbing at a frenzied pace. I'm afraid that I might have misjudged where the good investments were when I bought into San Francisco real estate. Now with the earthquake, I doubt I will see a profit any time soon. But I can't complain, since there was no damage to any of my houses in the Richmond and Sunset. Actually, I was told that the block where I'm building the studio was unaffected by the shake due to waves that cancelled each other—pretty crazy!

Also, for the first time, I realize how much people have changed since the old days; not as much in their looks as in their mannerism, as if something playful had left to be replaced by an awareness of social responsibilities, which is neither good nor bad. It varies based on personality; as to some, responsibility translates as being more cognizant of one's place in the collective, to others, it's more of a slant towards aging the cynical way, or more specifically, the fear-based way.

You'll often find the latter category reminiscing about the past as the good old days, suspicious of a future full of ambushes, where the body in particular is seen as the troublemaker—the traitor for pushing health and vitality out of the way. I have to say that I find this rather ironic in the face of all the shit these people put in their bodies, from junk food to unjustified doses of pharmaceuticals, and not to mention, the ridiculous amounts of alcohol and the chain-smoking. But above all, I'm mesmerized by their blindness to the very belief systems that perpetuate their cynicism; and let's be clear about it, they're the first one to bitch about life and call the mindful and health-conscious lucky. As if!

In the end, it's difficult to remain friends with those that fall off the path of vision. I can only hope the best for them, and who knows, people may surprise you!

I'm aware of sounding like an elitist when I speak about others. I admit to be one in the sense that I cater to my personal views as something worth putting forth. After all, who's gonna do it for me? But to my credit, I'm not attached to being right, and certainly OK with being wrong, since neither can provide a proper marker to truth. We just juggle estimates at best. The system of beliefs is the biggest managerial task one faces in life. To put it mildly, it's a maze full of screens and mirrors on which the outcome of absolutely everything balances. The most amazing thing of all is that we build our own from the ground up. I'm sure there's a universal template somewhere, but I haven't seen one. Mostly, we get ours handed over by the old folks and it's up to us to sort out the bad seeds before we venture into growing our own.

I can attest to the task for having removed a shitload of my parents' garbage before I could make sense of that template. I hope you follow the narrative.

For the first time, I get my sisters and brother to visit London together. They all stay at the house, which is thankfully big enough to accommodate us all, although it's tight around the bathrooms, especially with Wind and Muse, who, when they need to go, means they need to go—now!

It's nice to all get together, but I have to say that the biological family is only as strong as one's willingness to make it part of the extended one. Gene bonds can come loose with time and the lack of emotional connectivity. I can tell, with my siblings, that we could have benefited from spending more time together firming up those bonds. But no-one's to blame; actually, blame isn't even part of the equation—it is what it is.

Lisa makes sure everyone's feeling the love, and believe me, she doesn't have to try. As it turns out, everybody loves her, to the point of me catching my brother looking at her as if he wished he were in my shoes. I find it both amusing and endearing. Lisa's a Goddess in every perceivable way, so who can blame a guy for noticing!

Actually, my brother is the only celibate in the house, since my sisters are married with kids. It may seem odd that none of their partners and children are here, but school and work schedules aren't permitting. Eventually, we'll arrange for a big family reunion, either in the States or France. Moose at some point suggested bringing them over to South America, but the logistics don't lean in the idea's favor.

It feels great to be back home, even if San Francisco is still in shambles from the quake. All of my properties and equipment are fine, and even if they weren't, it wouldn't be the end of the world. Too much sentiment around things anyway, same with the past—no need to let it crowd the present. Things and past, I know, no relation, but there is one—*staticity*, even if it's not a real word. You may say a car, a thing, isn't static, to which I argue that a car is incapable of operating on its own, thus, devoid of an operator, it is left to rust on the street. Things are only non-static when they're connected to a dynamic motivator. And the past, well, it may be active in its own present, but not necessarily when it only exists in the form of memory. That's the kind of past I'm talking about, not the present past. I'm sure you get it!

So, being back home feels great, especially so when the twins exhibit their excitement—they know where home is—and it's all the more accentuated by the fact that they've been missing Nonna.

The Marina's a total mess—a war zone. So many people have lost their homes, their raison d'être; it's pure tragedy. We help the best we can, volunteering for cleanup, joining fundraisers, donating food... the responsible things to do when we all need to join elbows. It helps to imagine what it would be if roles were reversed, to be left without a thing, no shelter, no point of reference, and a future that keeps radio-silent. A big part of empathy is understanding how much we all need each other. Love for one another is at the base of it all.

We don't stay long, for we have to return to Argentina for my *regular job* which is now more tea than music, but it's all relative since I see artistry in anything I touch. No, I'm not quitting, just taking a step back for the sake of better perspective. I still do quite a few sessions here, as well as in London and recently, Brazil, which is probably at the level of any guitarist's dream job, but compared to the days of touring, primarily around the first two albums, it's a lot quieter. Moose, friends, and I are all fired up for the next album of jungle noises, but this time around we have some very special guests; one old mate of

Moose's from England, John: on bass and horns; a great pal o' mine from S.F., Mel: on the Hammond B3; and Mel's project partner, Steele: on drums, whom, amazingly enough, I met at *Surrey Sound Studio*, in Leatherhead, while his band was recording their first album way back when—small world! I sense this one might be the real thing.

I try to get El Jay to join since he's in the neighborhood, but as it turns out, not all in the music biz are best friends—stuff that goes way back but that doesn't want to heal. It's true that El Jay can weird out some people, although the reasons escape me, since he and I took a liking for each other the minute we met. But I don't mingle with the stuff that belongs outside my area of control, plus no-one can truly get to the bottom of what really goes down. It's best to not ask questions.

The album which goes by the title of *Tea & Jungle Noises* does well indeed, putting, in the process, *Criminal Records* on the map of visible indies. It's a small achievement, but it means something to me.

So when I say tea overtakes music job-wise, it's all a figure of speech. Tea actually provided the stimulus to go ahead, and I don't mean to pun. The setting did it, and I hope it'll do it again soon!

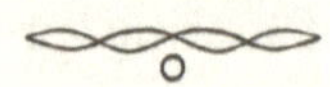

19 – SÃO PAULO

Moose and I agree that our time as tea partners is coming to a close. We give ourselves a year before pulling out of the business. We had a good run, but we're both antsy to get back to civilization.

Lis and Kay are with us on it. It's not like we don't enjoy the lifestyle, but we all come from big cities, acceptant of the fact that we can't shake some level of culture out of our systems, because, honestly, we don't really want to. Neither Lisa nor I are ready to abandon our nests in San Francisco and London, plus we want the twins to go to proper schools. We deem their wilderness education advanced enough to protect them from the bullshit embedded in our public institutions. Just like Moose and Kay's kids, "cousins" Ames and Jess, Muse and Wind are wise beyond their age. Talking of Ames, she's been running the roost, although telling it doesn't come close to describing it. All this to say, what a delight it has been living near those guys, and regardless of where we end up landing after we close shop, I hope it'll be within easy reach of each other, maybe even in the same town. Wouldn't that be great!

Moose and I are on business in Brazil—São Paulo to be exact. The Goddesses decide it's a good opportunity to do some shopping in town since we're staying at the *Jacques Pilon,* a walking distance from some of the finest boutiques in South America. After all, it's been a long stint with the jungle and the women are ready to go wild! It's a beautiful day. The kids are staying behind in Buenos Aires with Kay's sister, so it's only the four of us.

Just as our divine spouses finish crossing *Avenida da Liberdade* on their way to their shopping adventures, and Moose and I wave at them before turning around to get to our business meeting, out of the blue, two cars come racing and screeching down the street from opposite directions, opening fire at each other—then they're gone!

We hear people screaming; there's commotion across the avenue. Moose and I run. Both Kay and Lisa are down, Kay with a hit to her upper right chest, Lisa with a bullet to her head, her hair soaked in blood.

The world begins to spin, it can't be! Moose utters something that sounds of total distress. It appears Kay's badly hit, and by the look of it, Lisa's life is on the line. My heart races to breakpoint, tears blur my vision—I lie down next to my love, begging her spirit to not leave quite yet. She's going through spasms; it's bad—I'm so fucking scared!

Lisa and Kay survive—two warriors wearing their indelible battle scars. Although, the bullet went through the bone, Lisa's left brain suffered negligible damage; the most invasive part having been the reconstruction of that part of her skull. Needless to say that at this point Moose and I get the message loud and clear—the game's over with the trade!

Now comes the time to let go of the bundled up emotional mess caused by the trauma that came crashing into our lives the day two drug gangs decided to go at each other. As Moose and I ran across the avenue to our gunned down wives, the charge was so massive that time and distance became lost in a flickering series of frames. The cognitive qualitative rode on all-up red flags, as we both saw a version of the worse case scenario play before our very eyes. At that precise moment, an accelerated aging process kicked in and didn't relent until it was assured both were going to make it. Time stole years out of our lives in that ill-defined wait, its gears slipping while everything slowed to a crawl. There's nothing more grippingly intense and traumatic than the loss of a loved one, even if only played through the hopelessness of fear. For that moment, the despair was sinisterly real.

Following Kay and Lisa's concurrent releases from the hospitals, we return to Buenos Aires to fetch Jess. Nearly a month has passed since the shooting. Two weeks ago Moose flew back to check on his kids. Ames was so distraught by the news that he had to bring her back with him. No wouldn't do!

It goes without saying that the mood is of a different color now that we've gone through the wringer—we all are emotionally exhausted and ready to leave paradise behind. Moose and family are temporarily staying at their ranch in the Sierra Foothills until making up their minds as to the final destination—there's talk of New York. At least we won't be too far from each other for a while, though I sense some distance might do us good. For now, it's a time of reckoning, of gathering the memories of our life together—the trade, the music, the sense of family. But not all deserves romanticizing over; the good times were intermixed with the cutthroat moments of the trade—it wasn't all play—and now that we went through extreme trauma, it's easier to see the picture for what it was: lots of work aided by family support and the fact we had the extraordinary ability to stay calm under fire. There are no regrets, only a triumphant sense of accomplishment—that is clear!

San Francisco is back to being its up-and-going self. Nineteen-ninety has been a year of reconstruction at the fundamental levels. I'm not sure, but there seems to be more Europeans is town than I've ever seen before—French, English, Scots, Irish, Germans. Pubs and restaurants are opening everywhere; and yes, the flow of Hong Kong money is starting to be felt, prompting me to buy the last two houses I believe I will ever be able to afford. Prices nearly tripled in the last three months, as people buy to immediately put property back on the market—it's insane! Lisa and I now own half a dozen rentals plus the studio. I trust it's about as far as I want to go with real estate, and frankly, there's nothing remotely redeeming having to deal with renters and the continuous issue of maintenance. That's why I hired Frank, a goodhearted, semi-retired Italian contractor and his right arm, Little Joe, to take care of repairs and remodeling—good men, often seen at the house with their wives and children, over fun and hearty dinners.

The Studio is doing fabulously, and though I haven't recorded there lately, it's been well used by local artists under the amazing skills of my new engineer,

Craig, who's a hell of a guy, fearless about using old and new gear in such unique ways, that I have now labeled his touch, the *Craig Sound*. I swear, the dude is adding mojo to the name *20th Avenue*. While Craig is technically a free-lancer, I'm confident he'll be responsive to my offer of a permanent job. But wherever the wind blows!

It's January of 1991. Moose, Kay, and the kids visit one last time before permanently moving to Manhattan. They're in the process of selling the ranch in the foothills and the couple of houses in the city, so it's clear we'll be forever separated by a continent, but I doubt we'll ever be truly apart.

20 – TIBURON

The little house on Telegraph Hill has served us well, but it's becoming increasingly clear that we need more space. Muse and Wind sharing a room is no longer in the realm of the practical among other things. But losing the place would come at the cost of relinquishing a lot of the magic that has helped towards the coalescence of our family into the tight, loving unit it has become. The one option is to turn the living room into our bedroom, but I personally don't see how that can work past the experimental stage. The idea of moving elsewhere is heart-wrenching; neither Lisa and I nor the twins want to let go of our little house on the hill.

But fate turns the tables around. As part of a large city planning project, our beautiful home is no longer welcome where it has lived for nearly a century. The big money, which I had foreseen would, one day, come to inflate the real estate market, is landing at our door with the equivalent of an eviction notice, aka an eminent domain piece of fuckery. It simply translates into a bigger fish claiming the neighborhood for itself; so never mind history when you can build a multimillion dollar condo complex on the spot of a single property. We could sue, but we are advised against the idea. Instead, the option is to move the house somewhere else—fucking brilliant!

And then there are the London properties. At this point, it's unlikely we'll spend substantial lengths of time in Britain. For one thing, I haven't had a call since starting the tea job. I mean, Moose's idea of minimal impact was another way of saying, "kiss goodbye to your musical career and welcome to the real world!" Of course, I went along well-knowing what was at stake, so no blame there.

It's obvious I should sell those two houses, since I hardly make any money on the rent because of the ongoing maintenance. And let's face it, people change under the push of times, ushering lives along their predictable courses, which in our case means different directions. I haven't heard of Neil in nearly two years, and El Jay has been too busy being a rock and roll star to bother, notwithstanding that I haven't made much of an effort to maintain old friendships. Lisa, the twins, and I managed to have that family reunion in France after all, but nothing much came of it; we all reverted to being semi-strangers to each other, increasing the distance, one falling of the leaves at a time.

Selling the Camden houses frees a lot of capital, affording us the luxury to buy a large property in Tiburon, with a pad ready to accept our love nest, directly across the bay whence it came—practically the same view in reverse! Now, one may ask why bother moving the house if it's too small? Ask no further, the property comes with its own dwelling, large enough for all of us to live in comfortably. The Telegraph Hill house is now the art studio. In a bizarre twist, the complex work of moving it wouldn't have happened without some unexpected help from the realtor that brought the property, and of course, the lawyer we hired to see through the legalese of City Planning.

Of course, we would have much preferred to keep the house in the city, but no parcels were available in the districts we liked. All in all, it took selling the two Camden properties and the money gotten from the city to purchase one house and move another. Not exactly the best of investments, but when dealing with Tiburon that's what you get. That being said, we love our new place.

Another thing that comes crashing, particularly in Lisa's life, is Nonna's failing health. It happens fast. One day after running her usual errands, mostly consisting of pushing her grocery cart from her house in the Marina to the neighborhood Safeway and back, she couldn't get out of bed, complaining of fatigue and pains in her legs. Let's face it, the woman is ninety-nine years old, and to have remained active to this point is nothing short of a serious accomplishment. What I'm saying is Lisa's grandmother is likely on her way out—it shows in the way she says, "It wasn't perfect, but no matter, I had a good life."

Lisa moves in with her, while the twins and I visit daily. Nonna gets to live another month before saying goodbye to the world. She passes in peace, in her home, like she asked for, and I feel proud for our little family to have made that wish a reality. Nonna was the world to Lisa—the emptiness is hard for all of us to bear.

Nonna and her husband were part of the Italian migration that defined North Beach. With her gone, it is undeniable that the place that welcomed the beat poets of the fifties and sixties is turning the page on its own history, and that the men and women that tended its stores, bakeries, sausage factories; those who played bocce on Washington Square on lazy Sunday afternoons while sipping prohibited libations made from grapes grown in small family vineyards along the Russian River, are now ghostly figures seen by those who connected with the past through their elders. Lisa is one who still sees their lives unfold as if time had been too slow at erasing their tracks. One may say that memory is the place where things gone are kept alive.

The kids love Tiburon, especially since we can board the Ferry every time we need to be in San Francisco across the bay. From where we live, we can see the Golden Gate and the entire city, and if it weren't for Angel Island, we would also see the Bay Bridge and Treasure Island. Angel Island is where we all take our bicycles on Sundays and hit the trails, a ferry hop away— life couldn't be any sweeter!

My job, these days, is to essentially commute between *20th Avenue* and *The Plant* down the road in Sausalito. While I'm in the process of recording another one of those albums that most likely will only reach a select audience, which is where I'm at philosophically-speaking, I strengthen my position as one of the Bay Area's in-demand session men. Sadly, most of my gigs are to sit with artists that will never go past the stage of demos, or at best, a self-produced first album. Everybody wants to be a rock or pop star, and with family wealth— especially in Marin—dreams are made temporarily possible in the exhilarating ambiance of the recording studio, where hearts pulse to the beat of expensive monitors and top-of-the line compressors. It may sound mean, but there's no meanness in the truth—it's just the nature of business in the competitive field of talent. I can't just shoot my means of making money, but acknowledging a continuous play on the theme of irony isn't forbidden—I feel comfortable with it.

It's different with bands since they're their own players, and, unlike the old days, they're all competent at what they do. I'm mostly talking about singers with the means to hire a lineup of seasoned cats to back them, but we can't provide the heart, just the necessary fire. In most cases, we know the outcome from the get-go; that's why we don't stick around after we're done laying our tracks.

Finally, I get El Jay to show up at *20th Avenue*, since he's in town for a concert with a one day break before hitting L.A. He insists on only doing rhythm guitar, which makes me the only one I know to play lead on his takes—I'm fucking honored. Since we can't put his name in the credits, he deems it safe to not stick out with his distinctive style. I think he's just kidding himself because nobody gets fooled by his touch, lead or not. But you never know, since he's been copied ad nauseam.

It's nice to get reunited after all these years, especially considering how much he contributed to me being where I'm at right now.

"How's that tea deal with Moose; I heard serious shit went down in São Paulo?!"

"Yeah, you heard about Kay and Lisa, right?"

"Heavy, mate, how's Lisa doing?"

"She pulled through like a warrior, but she's been getting recurring headaches since then. I'm sure you know what I'm talking about."

"Yeah, I'm with her—we learn to cope."

"As far as the tea's concerned, we're done with that gig. We had a good stretch, but I'm glad it's over with. Moose's back in New York, I couldn't convince him and Kay to stay on the West Coast."

"I'm not surprised, mate, we tend to hang out where our roots first tapped their water, for me it's Kent; it doesn't matter how much I love L.A."

"I wish I could say the same about France."

"Come on, mate, you told me you hated the old country!"

"I used to, but the times have changed me."

"Thinking of going back?"

"Nah, just the old nostalgia hitting every now and then."

That's the way El Jay and I end the conversation as he opens the door of his rented Corvette.

"Don't be shy and please visit one of these days; you know where I live!"

And vroom, he goes!

21 – THE TOLL OF TIME

I've been seeing a lot of Breeze King lately; it seems we can't show up at a session without bumping into each other. The band's fine but Spork left in eighty-nine, sold *The Cube*, and went in hiding. It must have been a few months after I last saw him before the earthquake. He didn't seem to do so well at the time—personal demons like many of us.

Actually, it seems personal demons are doing some precipitous damage in the world of rock and roll, as I see old friends walk into their last sunset, ashes, bottles, and needles in their footsteps. Over and over again I have come to wonder what in success is making the human soul seek its own demise. I understand the disappointment in finding none other than emptiness at the end of a tunnel of hope, but the story is as old as time, yet it goes on in endless repeats, birthing and releasing cynicism, malcontentment, depression, and the likes. *Confusion will be my epitaph – as I crawl a cracked and broken path...* You know the tune.

Yes, friends are going, and more and more will go, as the end of our expected lifespans near, yet we're still vibrant, but how does an old soul fit in the young of heart—it's all figurative, I suppose.

Breeze King is an exceptional guy on top of being an ace drummer. He's actually on the album with El Jay—I believe it's my best recording, followed closely by

Tea & Jungle Noises. I haven't chosen a name yet, maybe something like *Twin Tower Radio*, but somehow I sense it's already taken—I'll just pass it by Wind and Muse to see what they think.

It turns out *20th Avenue* is my most successful business. For one thing, it's cozy, unpretentious, yet the equipment is top-notch and the neighborhood is perfect, with tons of restaurants and Golden Gate Park a block away for the musician who likes to run or take a quick hike to loosen up between takes. Mel and Steele miss the food collective across the street, but that's the way the cookie crumbles in a fast economy. And fast it is with the enormous influx of wealth from Asia, heaving entire sleepy neighborhoods into becoming the next trendy place to hang out. So, I'm very pleased with the way things are turning out with the venture, nothing that could have been possible with *Calibration Studios* or *The Cube* at the time.

Talking of *Calibration Studios*, I learned recently that Neil couldn't keep the place going and had to sell following Fuzzy's lost battle with breast cancer—a fucking tragedy! My attempts at connecting were futile. It's possible Neil needs healing space, but I'm worried about my old mate—one of the best men I've ever met.

I know I don't speak much of the family in France. They're all doing well according to Mother, who calls on a regular basis. It's been nearly ten years since Father passed, and I wonder if he's still investigating curious cases amid the layers of the in-between. Hell, I'm sure he is, the bastard! But I say this with endearment, because where else am I gonna take it? It's funny how the past changes with a different outlook at life—a single bloody choice, and boom, roses from manure—incredible!

Things change yet remain the same on many levels. We age, buildings rise on the razing of old ones, say, but inside, at the very center of our systems of beliefs, both social and individual, we actually change very little. What is said about habits seems to apply to our deeper tenets—when we're not just accepting them as part of the inner decor, we simply forget about them while they keep on ruling our thoughts and behavior. It's something I observed at a very early age while in the throes of angst. Actually, climbing out of that pit of agony was what made me cognizant of the power of belief. The more you fear, the more there is to fear. That's why, one day, I turned towards the aggressor and asked, "Is that all you can do?! Pathetic! Come on, give it to me!"

Naturally, there was no answer; nothing came to make things worse. It's not that the panic wasn't real; it was that by feeding it, it was made stronger to the point of controlling the weather of my emotional landscape, turning the rising sun to ominous skies, and the star-strewed heavens to the deepest blackness of hopelessness.

Yes, I remember those days, like lives parallel to this one—each a present alongside the others—moving at the beat of their respective timelines. It may seem odd to see one's subjective experience in such a way, but with time and practice, it becomes part of the larger makeup of who we are, or who I am rather, for I don't expect my kind of madness to be collective, although there is mass madness in the form of recurring hysteria, such as the incomprehensible call for war and genocide. But I digress.

It's funny in a sad way, but each time I think of France, I seem to revert to moods of despairing greys, scenes of endless rain, of urban melancholia with ghosts rather than people hurrying along the city streets, entering and exiting shops in photographic blurs, folding and unfolding umbrellas against the devilish winds racing amid the stone and concrete corridors. It is akin to feeling the joy of pain, a quality better than no quality at all.

To be reborn in a different country, as I was in Britain, doesn't necessarily mean the death of the past, even though I tried with all my might to make that happen. You just can't do it, at least not while staying alive. A funny thought, *thinking* of it...

I don't have a good reason to be reminiscing about the passing of time; it's just a cloud, really. I have all to hope by looking towards the future with the twins turning ten and the joy of music ad infinitum. I am also starting writing short stories, mostly about bands, where endless material litters departed stages, dressing rooms, and hotel rooms following the carnage of drunken parties; stories of mates dropping their pants and whirling their weenies with one hand, while precariously hanging to the mic stand with the other; or tales of wild, naked females rubbing their yonies against my guitar, to the yelling of audience hysterics. Definitely not the stuff I want my kids to read at the mo. But there's a charming side too, even if it never strays too far from the mallet of censorship.

I'm thinking about the end of the millennium merely five years away, a time I thought I'd never reach from the standpoint of my teenager years. Hell, I considered twenty-four the age that defined the mark of a decent departure. Little did I know, then.

I'll be forty-six in two thousand—damn, time flies when you're having fun!

I don't know if living in the South American jungle has anything to do with it, but I feel drawn to a place where life is simpler, where nature and wildlife dominate over the noise of machines and the belligerent screaming of souls gone amiss. I'm probably yearning for something I don't really want or need, but it's here all the same. So, on a glorious Saturday morning, we all hop in the SUV and hit U.S. highway 101 north—destination unknown. It's our two week vacation, planned to be unplanned.

We go sideways to the west then sideways to the east, one side is cool while the other's hot. I love cool but it often comes with fog just like in Tiburon. Muse and Wind agree hot is pretty cool. Yes, of course, there's that—the next hour is spent laughing about the pun!

We all agree we like Eureka and Arcata, not to mention the giant redwoods we pass along the way. Arcata is the only American city I know of to have elected a socialist mayor, which is pretty radical thinking of it. Now, that's a title you don't necessarily want to brag about outside the progressive zone of *Ecotopia*!

I somewhat know of the area through *the Captain*, whom I met once in Arizona while touring with the old band. I'm thinking of swinging by his place a few miles north in Trinidad, but Lisa and the twins want to go east and catch the Klamath River road to Happy Camp. The gang's been pouring over the maps and pretty much dictating the itinerary, so when I complain it's, "Dad, you do the driving, we're in charge of the rest!"

Trying to counter with logic doesn't go anywhere, but I'm far from being victimized by the process.

It doesn't take long to become mesmerized by the scenery offered by the Klamath watershed of heavily forested mountains and quaint, intermittent valleys. We come to the small community of Orleans, where we book a cabin for the night. It turns out we're lucky; one of the reservations was canceled. It also turns out the owner worked at the now-defunct collective food store across 20th *Avenue* and is a good friend of Mel's—small world, people!

Since the kids love it so much here, with the goats and chicken, and the river to play in behind the cabin, we decide to book the whole available week, and call it the spot for the rest of our vacation. Now, we know where to go next summer!

It doesn't take much to straighten my head, but I needed the precious rest away from everything. This is perfect and the owners are simply awesome at advising us on where to find the best swimming holes along the Salmon River, and the easiest day hikes for the twins.

On our last night, we get invited to a collective dinner in honor of the joy of living and the company of good friends—it's the touch that makes all the difference!

The following day, on our way out, we make a two week prepaid reservation for the next summer— that's how much we appreciated our visit—thanks guys!

The drive back to Tiburon is a straight eight hour shot, save for the customary pit stops and a meal at the market in Willits. We arrive, exhausted, tanned, and happy—the best unplanned holiday ever!

So, yes, there's the occasional memory that translates as the toll of time, but if one looks towards the future, trusting that much good is still to come, one may be surprised how their life might turn out.

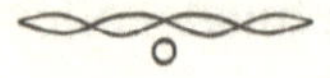

22 – TWO THOUSAND

We spend the new year's eve of two thousand in London where El Jay and friends are playing at an undisclosed club. It's kind of a private affair that is best kept under cover. Not that I care, but names can't be named because it would spoil the surprise. Rock and roll royalty isn't any different from royalty itself—just different costumes—the commons still eat cake. Which brings me to how and why Lisa and I are part of the guests if I'm gonna be so critical. I jest, of course!

I have pressed Moose and Kay to join us, but the offer has been turned down.

"You know, mate, the shit that went down with you-know-who, back when, is still stinking the fucking place up, so better that I stay where I am."

"So, you're never going to tell me what exactly went down?"

"You don't want to know!"

Moose will never tell, but, eventually, I'll get to the bottom of it. For now, we're here to enjoy the music, the food, and celebrate the approach of the new millennium.

I learn from Chrissie that Neil moved to Berlin, where he D-Jays for one of the monster clubs that are trending these days. He's apparently a hot commodity over there—good for him, he deserves the break! He's remarried to a respected avant-garde choreographer, an ex porn model who seems to know what attracts a crowd. Kudos to the two of them!

We swing by France to visit with family and a few friends from days long gone. It's a first through the *chunnel* for the twins, and also the high speed of the French rail system—the scenery is nothing but a blur the moment we hit the continent. It all seems novel, but those trains have been around since my high school days. I wonder why it took them so long to gain acceptance. I suspect the entanglement of bureaucracy being at the base of it, like it is at the base of all things that linger in the overstuffed *ins* of cluttered desks—something to think about when riding on a train at one hundred and eighty miles an hour with the family.

As I've already said, much has changed over the years, yet everything remains the same. It's likely that as we personally evolve in an ever changing world, the perceptual difference only becomes a quality of whether we're aligned or not. I hear people say, "Oh, you're not going to recognize the city!" Yet, as I see new buildings, pedestrian streets in the place of traffic jams, ancient structures gone, etc... I also see things being as they should be—a reflection of the times. So, in the end, it's a personal interpretation on the theme of better or worse, but on what determining factor—taste, opinion?

Speaking of opinion, isn't the term open to flexing under the weight of evidence? I hear that we're all entitled to our version of the truth; indeed we are, but what is the truth we speak of? I have one word for you: belief system. Dare change your beliefs and see how you create the world under whose rules you live!

I must be operating under the hypnosis of the blurred, flashing colors that pass us at ungodly speeds. Yes, that's how my mind works, in series of observations followed by metaphorical questions. I don't have real questions about life at large or the nature of personal reality; it all seems to be one big pot of potentiality better ridden than harnessed into submission. Lessons are rarely learned by the force of will, at least, the long-lasting ones.

Muse, who's always up for a question just when I deem it is better not to ask, seeks my opinion on why French cows have horns, while the English or American ones don't.

"I guess the French see nothing to being gored."

"Come on, dad, seriously!"

"I don't know sweetie, but my opinion is that it has something to do with safety."

"The French don't believe in safety?"

"Maybe they have a different way of looking at it."

"So, what you're saying is that all cows come with horns, right?"

"Calves don't; they grow later. In the States, farmers use big irons to burn the roots, so that they can't develop."

"That's barbaric!"

"Yes, we're barbarians."

Fucking barbarians we are! And hypocrites, and bald-faced liars to the one in the mirror! May I remind you that in an advanced society, a term like *collateral damage* would stand no chance to make sense. And *war*, people, does sanity stand for war? Do I need to take you down the rabbit hole of absurdity? Of course, we're barbarians! Let's just fucking admit it and go on killing each other, torturing the animal world, and destroying the planet! Yeah, I can be a cynical son of a bitch, but I ride my cynicism rather than let it rule me.

Alright, that ends my allotted crazy-thinking time—back to reality!

So, it's the year two thousand, the twins are fourteen going on fifteen, and while we age, the natural world around us is constantly reborn. Could it be the same applies to us, humans borne of nature. I've heard that every seven years, all the cells in our bodies are replaced. I very much like the idea and the science behind it. It suits me to think in those terms—circular lives within the ever-revolving wheel of evolution. One might argue that evolution isn't cyclic, but really, let's not split hair on nuancing. If I get the logic, we slowly die and get reborn over a period of seven years, never noticing. That's probably what happened to Father on a grander scale, he passed, yet he's still up to his old shenanigans— he never realized, or if he did, it didn't make one iota of difference.

I can't help thinking about what happened to all that knowledge we're supposed to be born with, the genetic encoding, the natural ability to walk, speak... Why is the body so wise, while the mind keeps searching? Pause for a sec and bring your hand, any hand, before your eyes then move it in a wave pattern, watch it dance and imagine for an instant how it does it. I don't think you can until you start asking the deeper questions about cellular intelligence, units of consciousness, and purpose. You probably think I'm crazy, but I can't help thinking about that kind of shit when my intellect is deprived of a project to distract it away from wandering.

It also means Lisa and the teens have left me by myself, to either locate the WC or the restaurant car.

We spend time in Paris. I tried to live there once before moving out of France permanently. I never felt more alien here than in any foreign city I visited or made my home. Even more alien than in the places I disliked most. Paris is another unexplained contradiction, for as much as I want to love her, she and I are in some way irreversibly incompatible. It's quasi-visceral. Every city has a smell, a body odor, comparatively speaking, and she doesn't smell right to me. It's not just the smell of piss— London and New York smell of piss too—it's the combination of all the scents that add to a final perfume. Maybe it's too much of a *Chanel №5* and not enough of an *Odeur 53*, if you get the analogy. But it's more than just scent—it's history that bleeds through the thin veil of time, the ever-present, ghostly past—and who knows— future. The enrobing ambience of Paris sticks to my skin and thoughts in similar qualities, stuffy and oppressive. Living here, all these years ago, was an earthly version of Hell. Today, it's just another place to visit—a five on a scale of one to ten. I mostly go through the motions, appreciating the appreciable, ignoring the abject, and guiltily drawn to the arcane without succumbing to the temptation—I just sense it because I lived here, but it's a forbidden unknown to those unwilling to fall for its hypnotic call.

Lisa and the twins are alright with Paris. Lisa's dad was born here, and we're on our way to meet with his cousin, an eccentric octogenarian always dressed in an impeccable, well-tailored suit.

Constantine's his name. He walks with a cane mostly used to point at directions and objects of interest, oblivious to the winter cold. We all speak French amid the French. We made sure the twins would be equipped to honor their dual citizenship, so we sent them to French schools in Marin and San Francisco—they're totally fluent in the language. Lisa's the only one with the accent, out of which Wind dares calling her *the ugly American*. He is quickly reminded that *ugly* loves the company of trash-talkers. He gets it—we don't find pleasure in making-fun within the family—we have rules.

Constantine makes me aware of what I have missed when I lived in Paris. He knows everything about the town, and I have to say that a good seller can persuade anyone that missing on the sale only leads to regrets, so I take advice and loosen up my prejudices. Of course, Paris is a gorgeous city, endowed with the benefits of an efficient transportation system and innumerable landmarks to discover right out of about every *bouche de metro*. But beyond the obvious, and just like all major metropolises in the world, it's in the intricate details that the true gems hide, and that's where Constantine comes in. The man never ceases to mesmerize with facts and stories, some long gone from the vernacular—some that even connect with San Francisco's own history, such as a tree planted by General Ferdinand Foch at the Palace of the Legion of Honor, or *Le Petit Trianon* on Washington Street among others. From where I stand, it only highlights how much smaller the world we live in is from what we believe, maybe not larger than the size of a walnut. Sounds nuts (ha!), I grant you that, but I'm fairly sure quantum physics can back me.

At any rate, of the few times I have visited Paris in the last twenty-five years, this has to be the best of the bunch; a tour fully orchestrated by Constantine, his cane, a baton calling out chimes and brass alike.

We leave Paris fully learned and at the edge of ecstasy. There is now magic where there was none, substance in the place of abstraction, forms pulled out of shadows, and a sense of joyful energy I never allowed to take hold, too preoccupied was I with the reality of pain. Constantine waves goodbye with one last arc of his cane.

Joni sang of parking lots paved over paradise; reversely, there is now paradise over what was once a three kilometre long steel mill, with a hiking trail going through the ghost of the lab where I used to work—a place that stock-piled enough poison to kill a entire major city and some. One could say that danger and safety, in their static form, have never been so close to each other.

Selling the wrong mill to the Germans may have seemed like an unforgettable mistake at the time, but to see the metamorphosis with my own eyes is the proof that with every ill, there is a counterpart, even if it is far from being obvious at ground zero. In the most tragic of mistakes and other catastrophes, rebirth follows.

I'm aware I could be treading dangerous grounds looking for a silver lining in sensitive places, but I didn't write the human tragedy, so don't read too much into it.

I can't quite say that the old province is finding its sparkle among memories, but I'm aware of improvement. It's evident the new generations are substantially nicer and smarter than those of my time, and the city's a lot more livable because of it. The enhanced environment makes for a fabulous family reunion, where it feels like its members have finally arrived at a harmonious convergence. I'm all for it—and damn, it's about time!

23 – ON THE THEME OF LOVE

Lisa and I celebrate our twentieth anniversary at no other than the place we met—Caffe Trieste—and at the same exact table. We wouldn't want it any other way. We're just back from Europe and the twins, their friends, and some casual supervision are in charge of Tiburon, because tonight, we're staying at the St. Francis.

It's been twenty years of a remarkable relationship, filled with so much love that it's almost a sin to mention it. But no need to be apologetic about love; it's a quality no-one should ever turn down. If it comes your way, you take it with all the humility and appreciation you can muster, never skipping a beat in returning it to its rightful place, for it's never anything you keep.

I have never spent a day during which *I love you* wasn't said at least once from each of us. Or if it wasn't said because of distance, it was thought with the kind of intensity that could practically be heard. I love Lisa with all of my heart and always will. There is no clause of unconditionality, no belief that says love must be present at all times—love is always there because we have arrived at a place where it is part of the makeup. It was here at this very table then, it is still here between us and around us, in our eyes and in the very fiber of physical reality at this fulcrum point. It is felt eternally in the essence of our mortality like a delicious paradox. Love is made stronger with time only because of trust, but when trust is there from the start, it remains the same, for it needs not be made smaller or grander when it only needs to exist ever so presently. Love is—period. Of course, it would be preposterous of us to make such a claim without the walking, but I assure you that we walked a solid twenty years on the theme of love—we know what we're talking about, and I don't doubt others recognize themselves in my words.

On this glorious Saturday, the 29th of January, 2000, Lisa and I, without saying it, engage in the second phase of a journey that will see us across the finish line victorious. It's kind of an odd way of saying that only death will take us apart, but since we don't believe in the unverifiable negative, we go for the positive one that takes us beyond that line into the great unknown as a team; in other words, in life and death we prevail.

Caffe Trieste is the symbolic first stop of our evening in town. It comes with the bit of nostalgia that there was once a house, a small distance away on Telegraph Hill, that belonged to us—our love nest as we called it. Of course, we still own it, but half the charm is in the location. Tonight, it calls again from its rightful place up from beyond a steep Kearny Street, as if to ask of us, one last time, to watch the city spread towards the setting sun. Dare I say that, on this special occasion, the past misses us?

Lisa and I, like a good many of the forward-thinkers, believe that love is at the base of life, that there is no desire to live without the touch of love. It's hard to imagine amid the rubble of devastation that love could prevail, but it does. It does in the heart of mothers, who if they didn't carry the flame of love, would be incapable of birthing children and provide them with their first nourishment—regardless of conditions. We all carry that flame to various degrees, but I grant you it's difficult to conceive of love being around through the ill-winds of pandemics, or the savagery of war, although tonight isn't the time for the mind to wander on the dark side.

Twenty years ago, a stranger walked into this very room asking permission to put her things on the chair across from me. She returned with a cup of house coffee, looking me in the eyes with a smile that invited universal love to sit between us. It was neither flirtatious nor was it the reflexive trademark West Coast symbol of free-spiritedness; no, it was the, *Hey you, the human across the table, what's your story?* kind of smile.

I was no-one special, for everyone is special. Suffice to say that not everyone responds equally to the presence of love between two strangers, but in my case it engages the sort of curiosity that begs to see through the question, and so it goes, *Are you sure you want to hear my story?*

Lisa was sure; she didn't ask questions she didn't mean to ask, and that was why she was ready for that walk down Columbus to the Wharf, and back to the doorsteps of her apartment on Greenwich for a goodbye assuring that the possibility of seeing each other again was distinctly open.

"What are you thinking about, love?"
"Our first time together."
"Me too, I knew I was in trouble."
"Same, but we played it cool, didn't we?"

"Cool was what brought trust between us."

"But we knew each other already, no?"

"Yeah, it seemed so—like a reconvening of old souls across eons that felt like yesterday."

"One way to put it, Goddess."

Yeah, twenty years ago that feels like now—that is *now*!—that is the always and ever—the timeless quality of love. We live it in these very words: we are forever! Guilty as charged, we go on to face an assured future of more courageous bliss and earned happiness. We dare to be naïve amid the currents of cynicism, distrust, and fear. We simply don't believe that the world was meant to be a sad place, so we make it in the colors of those chosen beliefs, that our universe is safe and that its power flows through our sacred selves—for you cannot love others more than you can love the one you are.

We're off to the same Italian restaurant we went to on my second visit to San Francisco, when the band was recording in New York. Miraculously, it's still there and we have reservations for a snug table for two.

The rest, as we both know, is history that cannot be relived—only continued. The now of this place in perfect harmony with the now of some twenty years ago, two points in time connected by an energy strand amid others in infinitude, emanates the same garlicky smell and serves the same Chianti in the grand cosmic style of the things that are meant to exist across the realms of the multiverse in unrestricted ubiquity. Does this make any sense? Ah, the complexity of describing a quality that may only be real in my imagination!

At any rate, we ride a high that needs not the help of substance, for love is the essence of nectar, the distillate of the sublimity of wishing to become, to learn, and to expand, and then to free the self of all desire, thus allowing the world to come into its own. But I digress.

Staying at the St. Francis may appear to be a weird choice—it's not exactly your love nest; more like a place for tourists and convention goers, like the big-hair blonde from Dallas who told me when I stayed there with El Jay, "You don't know fun till you've been to Dallas!" For some, the idea of fun is a big and loud everything, generally followed by a huge hangover. To each their own! But where was I? Ah yes, I chose the hotel because twenty years ago, on this night, I slept at the St. Francis thinking of the myriad ways Lisa and I could have ended up having sex. The signals were there, but so was wisdom. Tonight, we're going to make up for it since wisdom is now in our private circle!

I've always wondered about the difference between having sex and making love, if there is one at all. When I didn't know any better, I kinda thought sex was a cheap version of expressing love for one another, but I can think of the many ways of loving a first or solo date without cheapening the meaning of love. It's kind of a weird grey area. Maybe there is no measure of love, love in uncountable; you either open the door a crack or swing it wide open. It's a lot like light, or air you let in the room, no? And maybe the door works on the hinges of trust (ouch!). There's technically nothing to distrust in a healthy, new date, say, so all the glory of love can shine on the act of consuming the flesh and the exchange of bodily nectars. That's what I consider good sex, or good love-making. So yes, trust may have a lot to do with it.

Since there's always been a lot of trust between us, I don't have to get into the details of our deep connection at the level of love-making. Lisa and I like it straight up—no toys, no warming up to it—we're always ready at the same time, the bell goes *ding* and there we go! Positions vary more or less spontaneously, so no; we don't have a doggie night followed by the missionary on Sunday—you get my drift.

Anyway, I'm telling more than I need to already; the intention being on the theme of heart love, rather.

Lots have happened in the last twenty years; so much so that a book, under a deft pen, could be written about the two of us—about our love and unrestrained commitment to each other. I wish for all of you to find, if you haven't yet, that soulmate across the many veils of the mind and the deeper psyche.

24 – INCOME ALTERNATIVES

In the year 2003, we sell one of the San Francisco houses, which affords us to acquire two Victorian residences in the city of Eureka, and one in Arcata. Once again, I smell the winds of change, but this time, ominous ones. The reason for it is that after meeting with architects and building contractors alike, I've come to conclude something is out of balance with the market. In other words, speculation isn't adding up to my kind of math and the field shows what I refer to as a growing abscess. To put it more simply, the charts are based on the fact that the wealthy is stacking up on real estate, while first time buyers are burying themselves in outrageous debts disguised as easy loans, the kinds that get sold and bought in total disregard to all the red flags. It doesn't take a genius to understand what the financial edifice is cooking up. So, the game is, sell in hot markets and buy in lukewarm ones before something comes down. You may say that I'm part of the problem, but one knows small players are the ones that get screwed in the end—I just want to play smart with my hard-earned money.

There's something else the ominous winds are carrying: file sharing on the web. It's finally coming to the attention of the music industry that there is a greater villain than the CD-ROM format, which until now, required purchased material to copy from; no, this one's called downloading via BitTorrent, which translates as the fast, unlimited availability of music for practically free. The implications are dire and I fear the labels are slow catching up with the reality that their days might be over soon. But never mind the majors; artists are about to feel the brunt of not being able to sell music anymore—I can attest to it by witnessing dipping revenues across a dozen acts at *Criminal*.

So, it's why I and many others in the field are looking at income alternatives. Since I have an early start on real estate, it's a given I pursue the avenue.

Speaking of avenue, *20th Avenue* is also feeling the impact of change. Digital home recording is savaging the industry with the advent of cheap software and PC interfaces. While results may not be as good as those of a real studio, they're good enough to ears accustomed to low bitrate mp3s. And now everybody is a star in their own eyes, uploading horrid shit and clogging the arts' plumbing, so to speak. I fear it's only the beginning.

Back to real estate for a sec: a friend of mine owns a bank in Culver City. Back in two thousand, I told him there was something brewing that he should consider keeping an eye on. Yesterday, I asked him if he remembered my warning.

"What we're dealing with is something we've been waiting to happen for quite a while, especially since deregulation under Clinton. It's a big boys' game that promises to make a lot of money for the smart players."

"You're aware that the game will seek a mathematical balance, aren't you? Somebody's prone to lose in the end. You just can't keep on throwing money at buyers with shaky histories and sell high-risk packages to the next seller in line while inflating the crap out of the market, without consequences, can you? I'm telling you, if I were you, I would be careful."

"We know what we're doing; the market will eventually even itself out."

Well, I hope he's right, but it sure isn't looking like those guys could recognize *even* if it slapped them in the face. But I'm no financier, so what do I know?!

The third segment that is treading shaky grounds is the session business. It's not as critical as music sales, since many artists still seek help from seasoned players, especially the ones with recognizable names. It's a bit of a vanity game for those who can afford union rates, but it's played on a different board from the previous one. That's when file-sharing shows its good side, since digital tech crosses most recording platforms and can be sent via the internet. Now that remote sessions abound, the cartage issue has been practically eliminated. I just show up at *20th Avenue*, lay my tracks, sent the work through a large file carrier—money via PayPal—et voila! So far, still so good—just keeping options open. If I make it sound like music is business, it's simply because the minute you earn a living from it, it gets treated like a regular job—it's a profession that involves bookkeeping and tax schedules. Now, as we all know, music is also many other things, some countable, some not—like math and love. Much has been spoken and written about it.

20th Avenue has pretty much morphed into a complete production unit; a status *Calibration* and *The Cube* could never have attained. The days of demos recorded in top facilities are over; anyone can lay decent tracks in their bedrooms, though quality issues won't fool the trained ear. You just can't replace a fifteen thousand dollar compressor with a free plugin; that's the bottom line!

In perspective, the only real money I've ever made playing music was with the first three albums, which afforded me the luxury to buy the Camden Houses and the Telegraph Hill love nest. The solo recordings, as well as the *Jungle Noise* material, even though I believe they represent some of my best work, never generated much income beyond recouping costs. Let's face it, except for the artists on top, music needs a nudge towards related initiatives to remain sustainable; by that I mean, session work, endorsements, recording facility ownership, the things that still ring music even if they take you away from the creative field. As one of my close friends and guitarist extraordinaire would say, "It beats driving a cab!"

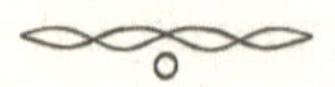

25 – CRITICAL TIMES

It's a big jump since the last entry, but I can't honestly say that much worth-sharing has happened. Yes, we saw the twins grow to reach their independence; yes, much music was played and recorded; and yes again, the real estate business has been good to me; but while things changed linearly, little actually did in the lateral realities—until now.

It's the morning of January, 31st 2009 when Lisa collapses on the floor of one of our North Coast houses. I am upstairs in the office loft when I hear her utter "Wowie Zowie!" As I look down, she points to the ceiling with both hands as if chasing butterflies with her eyes, and then, a scream—she turns blue, foaming at the mouth then falls off the chair onto the hardwood floor.

In the one second that follows, all versions of the worst case scenario play on the flickering screen of my panicked mind, frame by frame. By the time I reach Lisa, she is in the process of swallowing her tongue, unable to breathe as her body becomes a mass of taught muscles— there is not doubt in my mind that I'm losing her. I force my fingers between her teeth to reach for her tongue. Miraculously I succeed, as she, at once, noisily inhales and exhales in sickening gurgles.

The ambulance takes her to the closest hospital where a CT scan reveals a large tumor on the left side of her brain, in exactly the spot of her injury, where she was hit, nearly twenty years ago, in the São Paulo shooting. Oh my, that's how it plays at the tip of the baton of the conductor of the Devil's orchestra! A slow-motion bullet taking two decades to inflict the damage—please, maestro, lots of timpani for the final scene!

Since we acquired the northern properties, we've been in the habit of spending a month here, mostly for the sake of decompressing from the energy of the Bay Area. I'm aware that a life in Tiburon shouldn't necessarily require decompression, but a lot of my work involves tedious commutes and nasty traffic jams—no such thing in Humboldt. While we keep the one residence to ourselves, the other two are rented to dependable, trustworthy families under leases agreeable to all parties. We could charge much higher rents to HSU students, but we don't want to, knowing too well that the quality of money is only as good as the trust in which it is invested. The fact remains that reliable renters are a lot less brutal on property than party-loving youth. Anyway, just explaining why we're in Eureka, since it's my first time breaching the subject.

Lisa is flown to Redding, where the procedure for the removal of her tumor is scheduled, but lo and behold, fate has it that the malignance is too large and complex for the facilities' neurosurgeon and her team of anesthesiologists to tackle. They refer her to Stanford, while making sure to pump her full of steroids and anti-seizure medicine she's massively allergic to. Yes, dear friends, hospital malpractice is alive and well!

Within days of being back in Eureka, while awaiting scheduling at Stanford, Lisa falls into a coma.

Rather than call an ambulance, I carry her to the car and drive her to St. Joe's emergency room, where instead of taking urgent care of the patient, the two nurses in charge proceed to put us through the utmost in absurdity. First, I have to beg for a wheelchair to fetch my still unconscious partner in the car. Then, while I wrestle the recalcitrant main door, these torpid-brained ladies watch us struggle, not giving a fuck. But the coup de grace lands with their request to have my passed-out wife fill and sign her entry papers.

"She can't because she's unconscious!"
"Then she can't be admitted!"
"You've got to be shitting me?!"

I grab Lisa's slack hand, squeeze the pen between her dead fingers, and guide the fleshy contraption through checking the appropriate boxes and scribbling a caricaturesque version of her signature—there!

We're allowed into the waiting room, where we now must wait for half a dozen healthy-looking patients to go through their turn.

I take charge!

I call our family doctor, who calls the emergency unit, and before you know it, and to the dazed looks of the nurses, a gurney is rushed into the waiting room to take Lisa away. The two ignoramuses make sure to avoid my lethal gaze, but I have their numbers.

I did let the cat out when I previously said, "Medicine she's allergic to," and yes, the allergy in question is to phenytoin, an anti-seizure prescription known to lead to organ failure in some rare individuals. And by malpractice, I mean that the nurse in Redding saw nothing of the intense skin eruption over Lisa's entire chest area, which lists among the adverse reactions in the medication's critical side effects, namely: *a triangular rash over the chest area followed by liver failure and death.*

I could name names and blame places, but the self-imposed policy of these very notes forbids me to.

For now, Lisa is out of harms way, but Stanford's silence is getting me nervous.

It takes our doc a series of calls before the gears start to mesh at Stanford. Finally, a date is set as we prepare for the long drive from Eureka. Lisa is stable, but definitely out of it. It has taken her a week to complete a level-one jigsaw puzzle, something she worked on with unprecedented tenacity. Seeing her struggle through it practically broke my heart. She just looked at me with a loving smile, simply saying, "I'm going to finish this!"

"I know you will, love."

That's all I can say. Here we have a woman with a master's degree in social works and a PhD, promising to complete a thirty piece puzzle, as if she were in the process of climbing Mount Everest. But her determination shows there isn't a mountain too high for her to climb, or an ocean too wide to sail. That is the true nature of courage and it humbles the crap out of me. I am only worthy of her because I am her life support, otherwise, forget it.

Lisa's tenacity doesn't stop at puzzles; she also tries her skills at baking biscotti as per Nonna's recipe, but the milk has gone sour over our many absences, and she can't smell anything anyway because of a sinus infection she picked up at the hospital. I don't have the heart to tell her the baking emanates a foul smell. I bravely eat a few, but she admits that something might have gone wrong. It doesn't matter—it's the perfect biscotti.

Just as we leave Eureka, Stanford calls requiring MRI images in the possession of the Redding hospital, forcing a three hour drive in the wrong direction. It's unbelievable the shit these guys can put us through, as if the entire last month wasn't sufficient enough to have the shots mailed directly to them. The term *motherfuckers* comes to mind, but now isn't the time to jinx the process.

It's another eight hour drive from Redding to Palo Alto; not top for someone in Lisa's condition, but she braves the torture with admirable stoicism.

Just as we enter San Francisco over the Bay Bridge, Stanford calls again, this time to inform us that the surgery has been canceled due to a mix-up. As it turns out, they just realized they don't take our insurance. With nothing to jinx anymore, I just let the secretary know the extent of my English in unsavory terms. I don't think the title *motherfuckers* begins describing the kind of mindset I believe the entire Stanford administration has a patent on; lazy, irresponsible, and pathologically criminal are befitting adjectives to the term. I am truly appalled by what we are being put through—the sense that the entire universe is slowly caving under us is daunting. I did say that I wouldn't blame places, but fuck it; those cunts don't deserve my discretion.

We drive through the city to the Golden Gate, destination Tiburon. We have a lot of thinking to do; or rather, I do, since Lisa's brain is beyond the ability to think rationally at this point. For the first time, I feel the weight of ages, and I look it too.

Another month is spent trying to schedule the surgery at UCSF; it's like defusing a bomb to the tick of the last second. When Lisa falls into her final coma, I make the call that seems to loosen the cogs of bureaucracy. I don't know what I say; it comes from another place, from one of power for sure, since an ambulance shows up within minutes to take my love across the bridge into the intensive care unit of the second-best neurosurgical center in the country.

But we're still days away from actual surgery—I stay by Lisa's side. Barely able to open her eyes, she whispers in my ear, "I'm sorry if my brain isn't working."

Right here, in this very now, comes the answer to a question I have asked myself over and over again, "Is the intellect the only tool capable of summoning environmental awareness?" Lisa, from the depths of a near-insurmountable handicap, irrefutably proves to me that consciousness needs little brain to make itself heard. I get it loud and clear—she knows I do, while the others in the room have zero idea about what's going on. They don't have the bridge of love like we have; a language of the heart that reaches across the deepest and widest of abysses. One may argue that the little cognitive functions that remain are sufficient to establish the stage for self-awareness, but it's not the way it works at the medical end; as far as the nurses are concerned, Lisa is incapable of making sense.

I shall let you in on another bit of info that traveled between us; while Lisa reemerged from her coma, she started moving her fingers with the intention of letting the nurses and the doc know that she was coming out of it. What followed is best described as absolute communication breakdown. What she heard:

"Oh my God, she's having another seizure!"

As the team knee-jerked their way into taming the malignance of rebirth, Lisa went into total mental distress, unable to comprehend the absurdity of the world she dearly sought to rejoin.

Please, someone tell me this shit isn't real!

The twins flew in from Paris to join us. They're both in steady relationships, but as Muse puts it, "Dad, it's only as good as we're willing to grow!" That's my girl! As to Wind, who plays bass in an established French act, he's involved with Neil and Fuzzy's daughter, Sophie, who he first met as a young child when we stayed in London, years ago. Small world!

Everybody's extremely concerned about Lisa's condition. Of course, we all remember the shooting in

Brazil and the trauma that ensued, but to find ourselves here, enrobed in the discomforting ambiance of its unforeseeable aftermath, brings our common bonds, as adults, to a state of urgency that was never experienced before. It's alien territory for our team caught in the clutches of the possibility of losing our matriarchal figure—the original Goddess. Muse is holding the tears without much success, leaning against her brother, seeking silent affirmation through that inseparableness of theirs.

Me, I can only observe from the standpoint of the deep bruising that has turned all the joy to numbness.

Amid the peripheral players stand a few from Lisa's side of the family, namely her sister, Ann, who flew in from Seattle. The surgery is planned for tomorrow morning and will last until well into the evening. We all want it to be over with, but time is known to slow down in the occurrence of heightened levels of apprehension, as in insisting on the must to experience the raw nature of emotional intensity.

I'm a walking anthill, my nerve terminals sensitized to the point of crackling. I drink more coffee than reason dictates, but keep the appearance of the cool dad with the strength to carry us through the thick and the thin. I don't know which one of the two applies to the moment, but either has its place—thin on hope, thick on tension, say; but no, we all do our best to stay on top of countenance and positivity. We're the tough ones! We're a hive consciousness greater than the sum of its parts,

Lisa still very much in charge of her place. She's not going anywhere any time soon. We know, because we do, that her scheduled exit time from this plane is nowhere near today, so we decide to take lunch at 9th and Irving down the hill from 505 Parnassus.

Muse, Wind, and I take a long walk in Golden Gate Park, from Stanyan all the way to Ocean Beach—its entire length and back, in other words. We don't invite Ann, because she's a bit off-the-handle with drama, and her self-assured paranoia is of no help here. We all love Ann, but not the persona she's become around her sister's misfortune. Our family rises out of the bed of holistic thinking; we believe in creating our own reality from the ground up, where terms like *victim, martyr, innocent, accident, fate,* or, *it's just the way it is* find little footing in our daily lives. We ride our apprehension like we own it, our fears with the bravery of hope, our pain with the understanding that it positions us in being better receptors to joy. It doesn't come without work; believe me, but who says work cannot be play?

I'm aware that my words border on arrogance to some. After all, the power of trust in one's belief system is a challenge to those who choose to remain blind to their own powers. I can't conceive of apologizing for being me, and Lisa and I have taught our children well that way. Those two are forces of nature, brilliant minds twinned to big hearts—we are beyond proud of them!

We get the call from the hospital as we walk out of a Burmese restaurant on Clement Street. Lisa is out of surgery and in intensive care. The three of us get allowed in at 11:00 p.m. The Goddess is wired to so many machines that my mind goes into a spin. Her heart rate is at a steady one hundred and twenty beats per minute, which, as we are told, is a factor of pain. Her head looks liked a large bowling ball from all the bandage, her eyes, peeking through it, are ringed in red and black, while a drain tube protrudes from the base of her neck. She's an angel mended after a bad landing, a warrior stitched together from injuries suffered in battle. She's far from being the victim of a fateful, slow-moving bullet—she's still in charge, irrespective of the appearance.

I visit solo in the early morning. Lisa's partially aware; I say, *partially*, because the medical team believes she's not, but she lets me know, in a low whisper, that the night nurses have been mean, saying bad things about her while making fun. I believe her, but besides me and the twins, nobody else ever will—you just can't build a case on the wild imaginings of a brain-damaged patient, right? I'm just going to let it slip, but I'm pissed at the nurses nonetheless—this partner of mine is ten times the women they'll ever be—grotesque!

Just when things couldn't get any worse, the surgeon was unable to remove the entire tumor; and thus, Lisa has to go through radiation treatment; a five week process that requires her to remain at the facility during that time. The tragic part is that her pituitary gland is in the way of the rays and will die, which will require of her to be on hormone meds for the rest of her life. That, my friends, isn't our idea of holistic healing and something must be done about it! Just imagine for a sec where both of us come from; Lisa's a psychic healer and I've been immersed in psychic work for most of my adult life; psychic meaning something much different than what most are accustomed to. I'm not talking about spooks, or whatever séance mumbo jumbo, but about spirituality and the true empowerment of the self. Are we not all gods and goddesses, I ask!? Of course we are; it's just a matter of having the courage to admit to it, and with it come unbelievable deeds.

OK, you're gonna think I'm full of shit and just making this up, but no, call me a hopeless optimist if you wish. Just imagine that said pituitary (check you medical encyclopedia for definition) is tuned to a particular color, in this case, an iridescent azure blue, and that, should you surround the gland with it, a shield would thus be created against the deadly rays, just enough for it to survive the daily fifteen minute bombardment—just working from deep intuition, friends.

I pass it by Lisa who's all for it; so, the two of us, she in San Francisco and me in Tiburon, at exactly one thirty every afternoon, and for five weeks, visualize a protective blue light around the sacred gland. Not only that, we also suggest that the rays go around it and strike the area of the remaining tumor behind, just like water running around a rock in a creek. We don't waver; we just do it, doubtless and impervious to exterior influences. It's all about the love between us.

Since the hair on the left side of her head fell out, Lisa shaved the rest and now looks like either a punk rock singer or a mystical figure emerging from times long, long gone—a goddess all the same! We have an appointment with the endocrinologist who has the verdict on the hormone situation: the pituitary is working as it should—no hormone treatment necessary. Mission accomplished!

The radiations weren't supposed to affect the area of the brain that got zapped; so yes, we saved the gland but Lisa doesn't come out the same as the one who entered—something is happening with her short-term memory, and I'm afraid that the rays did substantially more damage than we were told they would. Had we been prepared, we would also have tried to protect that area as well, but perhaps it was too much to ask of ourselves, all empowered as we might have been.

It's reasonable to say that it's beyond our skill level to work on more than one miracle at a time...

The twins have returned to Paris; the good thing is that Wind is coming back with the band to record at *20th Avenue*, even though they have their own studio in *la banlieu*—a sweet way of showing he wants to be close to mom during her rehabilitation. Needless to say, the house will be busy for a while, and it's great to have the Telegraph Hill cottage as an overflow accommodation. Actually, it's where Lisa and I chose to stay—the original love nest in which we both found our true selves. It's the perfect healing space, full of extraordinary memories, positivity, and the sweet energy of years of meditation and yoga. My Les Paul Deluxe is still there, next to the old Princeton, still played, but rarely used for recording. I have so many guitars at *20th Avenue* that I can afford to keep this one close to my heart—we've been together for nearly forty years, same with the Fender amp.

This whole chapter is about ultimate inspiration, as I witness courage at its rawest. Lisa is fully aware of what she's lost, of what she will never be again capable of doing at the professional level—that of assisting the neglected and hopeless. Instead she will have to turn the compassion towards the self, love who she has become like she did those in the clutches of emotional and mental distress. She's still the healer and she's fully capable of resuming with psychic and energy work, but she's done with the battlefield of social psychology and the linearity of its methodology. She's left with potent lateral tools, deeply immersed in the intuitive, but no-one should expect her to accomplish the work tied to the cold logic of schedules, itineraries, or diagnosis, for she now possesses full control of the tools that belong to the holistic, the transcendental field of deep-base knowledge, the whole tied to the essence of love, a word, a quality that has been with us since the time we met, nearly thirty years ago.

26 – THE DAYS OF PRESENT PAST

Moose and I reconnect after almost ten years without speaking. I always wondered if my invitation on that particular New Year's Eve hadn't been the catalyst to the following silence. I misgauged how much he detested El Jay, all for reasons I have stopped inquiring about. Now it's El Jay's turn to be absent from my life, since he's ever the bigger star—practically unapproachable. I still know where he lives, and I'm sure he would be glad to see me, but with what happened over the last few years, it's difficult to reconnect with the past, unless the past is willing to connect with the present. In other words, if El Jay isn't calling, it's because he has better fish to fry.

So yeah, Moose and I are back on speaking terms, not that we had an argument to start with, but I sense that he was getting fed up with my closeness to El Jay, and that he couldn't bear dealing with what I guess he saw as total bullshit.

Kay's doing well, and interestingly, Ames and Jess have also settled for Europe. Time to arrange for the kids to bump into each other then! But Moose and I are seriously behind the times, since Ames' hubby, Richard, is friends with Wind's band via the guitar player, his old school buddy. The ridiculousness of the situation is best summed in Moose's own words, "Holy shit!"

Moose is horrified by what happened to Lisa. It's true the São Paulo fiasco wouldn't have happened if he and I hadn't had business to conduct in the city, but there's no redeeming value in going there—it was simply part of the programme. Kay is also feeling the side effects of having been shot in the upper chest, with recurring pains befuddling the medical field. In layman's terms it's called weather pains, most likely something to do with how the brain connects various levels of memory— another well-debated subject that fails at lifting the human mystery.

Even though I'm keeping all the analog equipment in top shape, *20th Avenue* has gone fully digital. There's this big ongoing controversy about the two technologies, their advantages and lacunae, but mostly it's in the perceived nuances that the debate rages. While some claim the ability to tell the difference, I personally don't care. I offer both indiscriminately, and if a client wants to shell the cost of two inch recording tape, something in the neighborhood of three hundred bucks a pop, I have the Studer for that. Ultimately, it's all going to the dogs from that point on, unless it goes from master directly to vinyl, because, otherwise, it'll end up coming out of someone's iPod, or other shitty mp3 streamer. At any rate, if I hadn't thought digital added major advantages to the recording process, I wouldn't have invested near five hundred grand into it—the main reason why I had to sell one of the north state houses.

It's not that we didn't have digital capability before that—we did in the smaller studio B, which I used for Skype sessions and various collabs that necessitated file sharing, but I had never recorded an actual album with the medium. Now, I am in the process of putting my next project together in the new A room, and I love the sound of it. To the Luddites out there, you haven't heard digital unless you've tried top of the line converters and clocks, and keep in mind that the entire front end and mixdown processing is still pretty much analog. But that might be preaching to the unconvertible.

So, in recap, the analog recording gear is now in an enlarged room B, and we built a new space for the small Skype studio, which is now C.

Lisa and I are trying to figure out a way of managing our properties more efficiently. It could be that we have too many houses, and now that the market has somewhat recovered from the two thousand and eight fiasco, we decide to sell the two remaining properties in Eureka. They are too far away, and even though we thought about it for a while, we don't plan on relocating there. It would be very hard to replace what we have in Tiburon, notwithstanding its easy access to West Marin, which we are particularly fond of.

Real estate is no longer a buyers market—it's actually stagnating at both ends. We're lucky to be able to sell those north-state residences, and because we bought them at the right time, we're actually making some money on them. I'm proud of having been able to smell the winds with my purchases and sales, while staying clear of the frenzy and greed. I've looked at them as rational, accrual investments based on personal observation of the market and global economy. I believe their value is now locked for the next ten years—after that, I kind of prophesy a major shift that may change the whole picture, but not until two thousand and twenty, at least. By then, accumulated wealth may not mean much, especially money. But I'm ahead of myself.

Every year, more people die, but I'm not talking from the standpoint of an increased population. No, more people die because all those we know have grown older, and lifestyles in the business, being what they are, most of us don't live that long. Oh, we acted like we would go on forever drinking insane amounts of booze and snorting yards of coke, but the human body is only made to sustain itself under minimal abuse. I'm being candid about it since we all seem to avoid talking about the obvious. The enemy isn't liver or lung cancer—it's all the crap that goes in, physically and mentally; it's the carelessness, the negligence towards loving the self. But I'm leaving it at that since I already have enough animosity looking my way. This being said, I'm nothing special—I just want to see things for what they truly are, that's all.

Moose and I have never been big drinkers, or heavy users of anything for that matter, at the exception of when our women were shot down. We like good weed, even though I've scaled down quite a bit, and perhaps, we get high on clarity and being creative, be it through writing, playing, or simply approaching life from a unique stance. That's why we probably will outlive our fifties and mid-sixties. Of course, there's Keef, smoking death away to disprove me, but he, along with my indestructible mother are the exceptions rather than the rule. Talking of Mother, I hear that she has taken a liking to scotch as a chaser to prescription and counter-prescription drugs—all eight of them as of lately. It also explains why, according to my brother, what was thought to be dementia is nothing more than hallucinations brought forth by the creative mix. I guess the doc will have to find yet another pill to offset the side effects, since the whisky is also prescribed for Mother's heart, albeit in lesser dosage, I suspect.

So, Moose and I have been reminiscing about the departed friends, the geniuses and the misfits, those fighting against the odds on their slow climb amid the stars that came down burning in a rain of ashes. I think I can invent more metaphors on the subject than in any other category. Rock and roll is full of bright colors that blink and buzz even after the plug has been pulled. We fill the gaps with stories, memories of greatness, achievements, of special moments that brought the masses to the edge of ecstasy and occasionally beyond. We rarely say he or she was an asshole, or if we do it's often with the right touch of endearment, a giggly nudge in the right direction for the sake of polite honesty. Although I can't obviously speak for everyone, because believe me, some have been buried with a shovel of coal tossed over their dead bodies, but those, we won't bother unearthing their bones. The extreme narcissists always die alone, rarely leaving anything behind. For those, time is like a windshield wiper—a few streaks then it's over.

But there were real characters among those friends; big mouths attached to even bigger hearts, the comics, the dramatists, the guys that made you feel safe, and the ones that brought you dangerously close to the forbidden... They would call you onstage when you were just trying to have a quiet drink, expose your camouflage, denounce the guise—we loved them for that. They all belong to books depicting the fantastic, for they were fantastic—giants in what they did because they didn't just do it well; they did it with grand gusto and total abandonment. They inspired!

27 – THIRTIETH BIRTHDAY

The twins return to California—it's official! Muse is bringing Jules, her boyfriend of five years, with her, while Wind, Sophie, as well as the rest of the band—their tribes included—are giving San Francisco a try on my recommendation. Two of the Richmond houses are reserved for the occasion, and *20th Avenue* will be made available to the musicians—at family rates, of course.

We're a week away from the twins' thirtieth birthday and we're having a bash at the Tiburon estate in their honor. There will be music and the whole neighborhood is invited. Because the date falls on a Wednesday, we arrange for the party to happen on the afternoon of Saturday the twenty-fifth. We reserve the evening of the twenty-second for a dinner for six at a special place in North Beach. It will be a pleasure to have tête-à-têtes with Neil's daughter, Sophie, and Jules, neither of whom we have had much of a chance to get reacquainted with since their arrival two days ago. The four will be sharing the main Tiburon house, while Lis and I will reside in the Telegraph Hill nest.

"So, dad," Muse queries, her usual subtle, "how does it feel to get old?"

"You must be asking because you're beginning to worry. Don't say no because I know you well enough to not wax casual about aging—you know I'm right!"

"I should know better, but yes, I'm getting apprehensive even though I shouldn't."

"To be honest with you, and it's something you should already be aware of about me, I don't really think about aging. When you look ahead like your mom and I do, there's nothing to worry about. Only regrets bring on melancholia and uncertainty. So, what's up with you at the personal, darling?"

"I don't know, dad; it's something that's been gnawing at me lately. I'm afraid to turn into something unappealing, no longer desirable..."

"Aren't you a bit young for that? You're in your prime, and haven't I told you a million times already that you're too beautiful for your own good? Is something wrong with Jules?"

"We're fine, but maybe that's the problem; we're fine without the excitement. I'm kinda counting on the move to shake things up."

"I knew it! Listen daughter, you're in charge like we've always taught you—if it isn't working for you, either change your outlook or the decor, but please, you deserve better than being depressed about aging!"

"Thanks, dad, I'll sit on it for a while. For now, I'm ready to leave the topic; I think it helped just being able to talk about it."

"You know you can always count on me, right?"

"I love you, dad!"

"Ditto, kiddo!"

A big hug and we're ready to move on—I'm a blessed father, what can I say! I've been missing that girl, and of course, I don't have to mention how excited I am to have the kids back in our lives—it's heaven on Earth!

Just as I turn around, there's Wind in the distance hugging his mother—it's a love fest at the ranch!

I leave a message with Moose to invite him and Kay to the party. They probably will rain-check since they don't seem to be traveling much these days except to visit family in Argentina and Europe, which by most standards is a lot of traveling, but I mean besides the family.

I get a yes answer—I can't tell you how much it warms my heart! On top of it, Ames and Jess are also coming, as well as their partners. As it turns out, Ames had it all arranged with Wind and Sophie! As if it weren't enough, Neil and his wife, Birgit, are also coming from Berlin, and Moose manages to get Spork and Breeze on the list as well. A good thing we have plenty of room at the estate!

At a few exceptions, the extended family is coming into a rare convergence, an event that definitely indicates that all is right with the world!

The birthday dinner centers on Lisa and I getting closer to Sophie and Jules. It's by no means an evaluation in the sense that if they don't meet quota, they're out. Ha-ha, no, we're not that kind of parents! It's not like we have never met them—we visited each other over the years. But it's definitely a check-up to see where the twins and their partners are at with their relationships, and of course, for them to see where we're at on our side.

Naturally, it's not something planned or even remotely talked about—it's a gentle flow within the nature of rapports that defines the particulars of resonance versus dissonance. In other words, it's not something one thinks about, unless that one is me.

Well, the main reason why I might be thinking about it is because of Muse's question about getting old. Otherwise, I would simply have gone through the motions more or less intuitively.

I don't have to concern myself about Wind and Sophie; the two have settled in quite nicely. As a matter of fact, they remind me of Lisa and I—an undividable team. But I have to confess that Jules is the subject of my interest. I wouldn't know how to probe him, but I can always observe from the crown molding in the upper corner of the room. Not as weird as it sounds, really, but let's not dissect the imagery!

Jules is quiet—more so than the other times we met—and I have to ask whether or not he's here of his own volition. I perceive sadness in him behind a mask of quiet countenance, the sadness of something irremediably lost. I wouldn't put it past my intuitions that he just ended an affair, or that a deeply private and rare opportunity slipped between his fingers. I wait for a clue—I know it will come. Meanwhile, Muse looks at me, not inquisitorially, but more like she knows what I'm doing as she expects me to be doing it. She's not my daughter for nothing—we can't hide anything from each other! If nothing reveals itself, I will have to ask her directly, but she wants me to figure it out for myself, as to not influence me—that, I'm certain of.

In spite of the task, I'm not losing track of having fun and staying sharp with whatever else is going on. I can multitask at the social level without acting halfway out of body. It's a lively group with much infectious laughter on tap, not to mention the kind of candidness only close ones can afford.

Muse: "Hey, mom and dad, what was the pose of choice when you conceived us?!"
Lisa: "Dear, we fucked so many times a day, how do I know?"
Me: "Based on your profile, Muse, it'd have to have been something wild—any idea Lisa?"
Lisa: "What wasn't, love?! All I can say, daughter of mine, is that you both turned out every bit as good as the love-making."
Me: "What's your and Jules' favorite?"
Jules: "You don't have to answer that, Muse."
Me: "Of course she doesn't, Jules! What about we change the subject—OK with you, Muse?"
Muse: "Yeah, sorry I started it!"

Et voilà, that simple! There's bad blood between the two and it's got to do with sex. Muse knows I've gotten it and she's now ready to talk about it—well, not in the very now as you already guess!

The party is insane! I'm all over the map with connecting and reconnecting. It isn't easy to be casual with such poignant emotions, to say, *we'll catch up later* when you feel like taking a side road and catching up now. But there are too many acquaintances that need their moment in the sun—so I oblige. Eventually, it's true that we'll catch up later. *Later* being an unassignable timeframe within a larger one, it brings me to wonder whether or not the party's long enough for that. Oh my, I'm getting apprehensive around not assuming my role with the proper management—how unlike me! But it's a special event that calls for rarely-used emotions; hence the mental disarray.

Moose and I don't need to get chummy since we practically talk on the phone daily, but it's nice to see Kay and their kids, who are now in their mid to late thirties. Ames and Muse are very much alike, wild and fearless. After all, they spent years growing up in the jungle together; and it's no surprise Wind took after Jess as well. It's also no surprise Sophie would be made in the mold of Muse and Ames, since Wind and his twin sister would be inseparable if it weren't for their respective relationships, which brings me to wonder how Jules fails at being closer to my son in character. Of course, by no means do I believe Jules and Wind need to be carbon copies of each other, but I'm running the harmony curve in my mind and I sense a dissonance, it being the keyword here!

But Jules is not the point of the party; he'll be around beyond it, with plenty of time to address the issue, should it arise.

My reconnection with Neil is of major importance. As much as I saw his daughter, Sophie, over the last few years, I haven't seen him in a long time. Neil was my best friend in London, and one of the few genuine individuals around when genuine was practically an item of emotional survival for me. He is a changed man in many respects, but his heart his intact. His loss of Fuzzy was something he barely recovered from and am I glad

Birgit was able to support him in his moments of despair, even years beyond the normal span of the *voidly* hell. He and Fuzzy were soulmates, something I've come to recognize the value of through the traumas of my relationship with Lisa. I can't fathom the extent of that despair, should I have lost her to that bullet or the ensuing brain surgery.

But in the end, I touch base with everyone, reigniting the fires of connectedness, rekindling passive memories into a precious present... We're not lost, we're eternal on our specific journeys, at times, distancing, at others, crossing. And if no time and space were to exist, let's imagine what it would be to come face to face with a complete unknown of even more radiance. The party was a resounding success!

28 - MUSE

Now comes the time to get down to business. The party was two weeks ago and my fatherly duties are calling. I know the timing is right by the way Muse looked at me this morning.

"So, ready to have the talk with dad, dear?"

"Was I that obvious?"

"Why should you ask when you practically begged for my attention? I know I could have come forward earlier, but I wanted it to be your call. I believe that's part of you training me to not nose in your affairs if memory serves."

"Dad, you well know contradiction's my middle name, but you're right, I had to wait for the optimum emotional crescendo before seeking counsel. Remember when I told you years ago, 'It's only as good as we're willing to grow,' well, the growth is in a state of arrest, in fact, it has been for the entire last year. The only reason why I haven't exploded is coz I believe I'm the problem."

"We've always taught you to take responsibility, so I admire you for that; but it takes two to tango, sweetie, so why don't you start with the beginning and see where it takes us?"

"Well then, a bit over a year ago I got wind of Jules having a flirtatious relationship on the side, something as you know I've been fairly open to since sex and I became good friends. So, after it was revealed that the flirting had turned into something far more lustful, rather than making a fuss about it, I looked at my options and figured that the most dignified way to operate was for me to also have an affair. But it's easier said than done since I like a bit of love with my sex, which makes me picky about whom I sleep with. I'm sure you already know where this is going..."

"I think I have a good idea, but please continue."

"Additionally, I didn't want it to be a reactionary response on my part, so I took my time, but that was a mistake. The fact Jules failed to share where he was at kinda sapped at the trust between us, and soon we stopped sleeping together, while I craved sexual attention and love. On one hand I shut the door, on the other, I locked myself in. I should simply have confronted him and gotten it over with, but I felt like I was betraying a common maxim, that of having an open relationship. Do you get it?"

"Muse, your emotions are in the way, but I'm following you. Remember, there's no open relationship if trust isn't there. The way I see it, he was the first one to undermine it by not telling you. I'm sure there are myriad reasons for him to hide that affair, but that doesn't make it excusable. So, what happened next?"

"Since I didn't seem able to find a willing partner, I began looking for personal issues. At some point, I started thinking of myself as too ugly and unworthy of Jules; I envied his girlfriend, but somehow and in spite of the growing distance, he still acted like he wanted to stick around, which confused me even more. In the end, I let go of the defenses and decided it was better to resume with the sex than isolate myself into alienation. After a few months at the game, I finally confronted him, asking him to explain why he needed that relationship when ours was perfectly fine to start with."

"I was wondering when it would come to it—I'm glad it did—so please, resume."

"Well, slightly after you proposed we all move to San Francisco, I offered Jules an ultimatum—either he dumps the bitch or he packs his bags. He tried to bring our contract of an open relationship to the table, not realizing he was setting up his own trap. I simply reminded him he had voided it by being a fake and a coward. It must have worked because he ended the affair and returned to the roost within a matter of days, apologizing to no end and crying profusely in the process. So, as you know me, I took him back, but it hasn't been the same as before. I don't think he stopped loving the woman, which brings me to, 'why is he here?'"

"Good question—what are his options outside a relationship with you? I mean he's a writer with a couple of self-published works of fiction, fairly good stuff, but without your support, he's a nobody. I trust you know when someone is using you or not, but have you looked at this for what it is? Am I too out of line to assume there's no longer any love in your relationship?"

"I didn't want to think I was being used until I spoke with you, but that's been the underlying sentiment for a while—you're right, he has nowhere to go financially without me, and more importantly you and mom, since you're providing support until I start work again."

"If you want my advice, get rid of the loafer; you've got nothing left to lose at this point, and as I've told you numerous times, you're too beautiful to not be loved! If you can't convince him, I can!"

"Give me a couple of days to wrap my head around it; I still have personal questions in need of answers, but I think I can handle this on my own. I know I always come to you and then decide I'm in charge, but don't ever assume that your understanding and support are taken for granted—I will always need you to pick me up and put me back on my feet! I love you, dad!"

I personally drive Jules back to the airport—he got the message loud and clear, and I didn't even have to intervene. When Muse is set, nothing can stop her, but as she said, the dude had built his own trap all along—in the end, he had nowhere to go.

But I'm not a beast and the guy needs a break, so he's got a bit of money waiting for him in France, and appointments with a few publisher friends in London tucked in his calendar. May he find his particular brand of happiness!

I mentioned that Moose had invited Spork and his wife Roxy at the birthday party, and so did he Breeze, my favorite drummer in the whole world. Well, as it turns out, Breeze's son, Forest, also a drummer, is doing a session at *20th Avenue* and invited Wind and me to join on bass and guitar on a couple of tunes. Muse, who insisted on checking the new layout, comes in as well. I don't remember if Forest and my daughter ever met, but it seems there's an instant connection, and sure enough, before you know it, the two are out getting snack food at the corner deli. When they come back, it's giggles filling the space and the kind of innate intimacy that only those who recognize each other can manifest—I think we have a match! And what an arrangement, since Forest is a lot like Wind in many respects! This comes from left field, my blind side, holy shit, life's full of surprises! I'm ready to bet Muse isn't coming home tonight—I can't wait for Lisa to get a load of it! I understand I could be projecting, but intuition is a powerful window into possibilities. After the Jules fiasco, I'm all for a fresh smile on my daughter's face. This makes me happy, because if Forest is any bit like his dad, she's in good hands.

As I had envisioned, Muse never came home that night, and now, two years later, Breeze and I walk the aisle at our kids' wedding. Once again, it's a huge party in the guise of a reception, where the regular suspects are all present, including my siblings who flew from France on my insistence. Before I lose tract of the sequence, we're not just marrying Muse and Forest, but also Wind and Sophie, who couldn't find a better time to tie the knot. What can I say—the twins will be twins!

Predictably, Moose and I stand to the side, timeless observers of the waves that keep on unfolding over the sands of destiny. Any better way to put it? Nah!

"I sensed it between those two a long time ago; why I never understood the Jules thing!"

That's Moose talking—the eternal visionary.

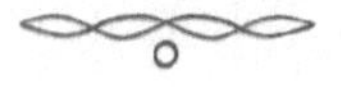

29 – COGITATIONS

The San Francisco experiment held—everybody's still around going about the businesses they've come to accept as daily life. Lisa and I are now grandparents to both a girl, Rose, and a boy, Everest, respectively Muse and Forest's, and Wind and Sophie's children. There are talks of the two families moving out of Tiburon, but we'll see about that—it's still a big house and we adore the company! We sold the two Richmond district properties to the band members at prices they couldn't refuse, and the world is a better place for it.

I just finished recording my thirty-third album right on time for the twins' thirty-third birthday. Just about everybody I know who plays an instrument is on it. At this point in my life, it's no longer about the money or the fame; it's about the art and the joy. There is enough drama out in the world to not relish what we have in the now of this beautiful existence, the one that radiates from the very center of this great family of eccentrics, free-thinkers and spirits, lovers, creators of their own realities, and above all, courageous souls that dare crossing artificial boundaries to reach into a glorious unknown. That unknown is a tomorrow free of fear and mistrust, a step forward without the apprehension of having to take one back; it is a place full of love for each other, one where the family keeps getting bigger as all of us humans and non-humans alike find our common ground. It is the stuff of dreams—my dreams, my hopes, and perchance, everybody's. I look forward to it, to that potential for greatness and accomplishments, and beyond, into the stuff of rebirth—the life given and the life taken. But once again, I lose myself in my natural high, the one of clarity oh so cherished since I crawled out of that hole of misery dug by my early years in what appeared to be a forsaken planet full of depraved souls, of war-ravaged minds, of hopelessness. How far I have come, or rather, how far we all have come, even if this world sometimes appears to devolve into apathy! It is by far a better place, like tomorrow will be, and the next, but only if we believe it hard enough. That's the catch, people, and though I hate to deceive, it takes work to get there. But in the end, it's nothing but a choice. Word of advice—don't kill the messenger!

Rereading my last paragraph, and to humor the self, I don't have to tell you what you already know. I get somewhat pompous at times—that's part of the duality within the self. Me, I'm my own actor and spectator—a tragicomedy of one for an audience of none. I'm OK with it—at the end of the day it's easier to balance the books. And the keyword here is indeed *balance*. I remember being born alone, with music in my head as my only companion. During the years that followed, that state of lonesomeness became more acute, as the world turned more and more into a picture of abstraction. To restore the balance, I had, in spite of the fears, to open the doors and invite others in. That's how the family got started. And look what happened!—I can't help but feeling proud. So please, forgive the occasional digression. Nonetheless, there's only one left in the mirror when the time comes to evaluate one's achievements and weigh the regrets. It's a necessary place to seeking the truth unadulterated. It's the definer of whether the work is a half-assed job or complete. It's the last place where a lie should find its footing and the only one where the field is clear enough to not have to resort to excuses for the failings. That's what I mean by being alone—to be in the private zone of the soul.

It's probably not my first time mentioning that *all has changed yet all remains the same*—a cliché for sure—but it's a matter of perspective. It suffices to look to the past as a point of reference to feel the full impact of change; reversely, when one looks ahead, the changes belong to the natural course, for there isn't any resistance in the path. The way I see it, change can never be bad—it only appears so when regrets are part of the equation. Each segment of the past is a step to the present, but nothing prevents anyone from deciding whether they want to go up or down. I'm the up-guy, crossing the many on their way down. The variations are nothing less than multitudinous travels on their specific destinations, but for the sake of simplicity, it's a lot easier to go with the flow than to fight your way against the current—time is the current, and change is the scenery that lines its shores.

So, as I revisit the past in my thoughts, the Camden properties, *Calibration Studios* and the myriad faces that traveled the halls of its big house, *The Cube* in the Mission, the Telegraph Hill love nest, the summer trips to the Klamath and Salmon Rivers, the Victorian houses in Eureka, the tea trade with Moose, the thousands of recording sessions, Lisa, the twins, the many friends, as well as the traumas and the millions of details that interlaced through it all, I cannot pretend that I have lost anything. All have been gains adding up to the present experience—a whole larger than the sum of its parts.

30 – A LAST LOOK

We're now in the year 2020. Lisa and I stand on the deck of our Tiburon house, looking towards San Francisco. There's a pandemic out there and the city is in lockdown. There are no sailboats on the bay, no ferries, no cruise ships full of elders and honeymooners on their cutout journeys. The silence is notches deeper than the one we're accustomed to, rendering the sound of the breeze and the call of seagulls hyperrealistic in their presence, all natural noises being now closer, more intimate, and also more startling. We relish the moment, as we imagine a world of far fewer inhabitants, perhaps as the way it was a century or more ago.

What will happen of this Earth when all returns to normalcy? Will we awaken more learned, compassionate, and understanding of the fragile social reality we have made for ourselves? Or are we going to forget once again, until the next scare comes around, this time, maybe something truly dangerous and *apocalyptic*, as the news corruptively endeavor to call this one... We all have our views and ours are probably more radical than most due to the fact we have long understood that we are in charge of our own lives. We have venerated our bodies like we have oceans, forests, mountains, and skies; put our trust in the healing powers that abound within our reach; sent and received love from the earth and the cosmos, from our inner beings, the spiritual, the unknown reality; put our trust in what we believe is true, even in the face of a lack of immediate manifestation, but it was worth the wait. All along, it has been a journey lined with love and joy. Oh no, I'm not saying that pain was never felt, that tragedy never struck the sanctity of that bliss, but all in all, that love and joy have prevailed as the dominant forces in our lives.

What we receive, we send back into the world through support towards those in need, via the arts: painting, music, writing... through meditation, prayers, and thoughts. And it echoes back, waves that crisscross space, ripples that undulate in semicircles to and from unknown shores.

We look at a reality with limited outcomes, two predominant ones. There is no in-between, no wiggling room—no margin of error. The choice is here, right now, in an ever so narrow present. Is the power of love sent from myriad places across the globe in this very now, powerful enough to tip the scales towards healing? We believe so—we believe it has everything to do with it whether you believe it yourself or not, because we trust there is enough goodness in all of us to help us come to our senses. We don't fathom the human soul is tainted by evil, in fact, we don't acknowledge evil as being anything more than the most basic manifestation of our fears. There's nothing there but an invented, religious spook—a harmless character in a Death Metal fantasy.

We believe that the love we have shared, consumed, and created with expanded vitality will change the course of where we have arrived, at this standstill in history, at the fissure of political and business edifices, as well as the rise of holism, the belief that the whole is greater than the sum of its parts.

There is something grander than ourselves, and when we think we have come to comprehend what that whole is all about, there is something even more majestic. It is a something we cannot evaluate from the subjective standpoint of being a cog in all that is, we have to become that whole to understand it, and yet, Lisa and I know that it's not where it ends, for that plenary is made greater each time a mind comes to rejoin its righteous place in the grand amphitheater of the spiritual.

But never mind the metaphors; we stand here sending our best wishes into a future of rebirthing and prosperity, for we want our children, grandchildren, and the numerous generations that follow, to thrive in the greater collective. We want science, art, and philosophy to meld into a creational force, and above all, we want all to experience the bliss of cohabitation, where all species find their harmonious role and purpose in the expansive makeup of the physical, the point in time at which we can all call ourselves creators of our own.

Lisa and I bring our bodies closer. Together we are indeed more than the sum of our individual selves— somehow, it's something we've always known.

So, not bad for having landed in the wrong place to start with. Just to prove that the power of choice can be a useful friend in a pinch. You know what I mean.

END

OTHER TITLES BY
THE AUTHOR

The Disappearance of Olaf Swyndle
(Book 1 of An Improbable Emergence)

The Hektor Dilemma
(Book 2 of An Improbable Emergence)

Ma-l's Grand Gathering
(Book 3 of An Improbable Emergence)

Convergence of the Realms
(Book 4 of An Improbable Emergence)

Escape from Inconsequence

Reyes & Leeds

Story of a Tale-Maker

Nine Amber Pieces

francisvoignier.com
Dolosse & Writs, Eureka, California